Tails From
The Country Side

BY DEBBY SCHOENINGH

To Marcia,
Hope you
enjoy the
"Udda"
Side!
Debby
Schoeningh

Library of Congress Control Number: 2003099010

ISBN Number: 0-9746360-0-2

Published by The Country Side Press
P.O. Box 34
Haines, Oregon 97833

Cover drawing by Marge Brown
Photography by Debby Schoeningh
Edited by Lisa Britton
Printed by Lightning Source

*T*his book is dedicated to: my husband, Mike, the love of my life who never fails to make me laugh; my son, Jake, my pride and joy whose smile lights up my world; my Mom, Helen, for her unwavering support, encouragement and friendship; my Dad, Perry, for teaching me two of the most important things in life — values and honesty ; and to Pete and Donna for making the ranching life possible.

In loving Memory of Skippy

1995-2003

Acknowledgements

I am especially grateful to all of those who encouraged me to put my columns into a book and to those who assisted me with this endeavor: Lisa Britton for her expert editing abilities; Ron Brinton and Doyle Perry of *The Record-Courier* for giving me the opportunity to write my column unabashed; David Asson, author of "Bringing In The Hay," for his book publishing advice; Carolyn Kulog and Betty Kuhl of Betty's Books for the gift of books on self-publishing; Dean Brickey, my writing mentor, for his friendship and advice; and all of you who continue to read, laugh and sympathize with my adventures as a ranching wife.

As I believe all things come from God, I humbly acknowledge His presence in all that I do.

Special thanks to Jake for always lending a helping hand on the ranch so I can write, even when he's dressed up with places to go.

Contents

Rural Communication

I've recently decided after talking to neighbors and friends that communication between husband and wife — although seldom discussed — is a growing problem among rural ranching communities.

You know the kind I'm talking about, like when your husband comes running up the lane behind a herd of galloping cattle and yells at you to open the green gate. Looking around, you see that every gate within a four-mile radius is green.

After years of stressing over this situation, I've finally gotten to the point that I just grab the nearest gate and fling it open. After all, action — any kind of action — is better than none, right? It's kind of like taking a multiple-choice quiz and nine out of ten times it's the wrong gate. He carries around a game show beeper in his pocket: buzzzzz, you lose. "I'll take blue gates for $100, Mike."

Or what about the dilemma of trying to help your spouse back up a trailer? For some unknown reason God gave men and women a different set of backing-up hand signals. Things always start out smooth, and inevitably fall apart at a rather rapid rate.

I'll be doing what I perceive as an excellent job of trafficking, telling him to go left, then right, then forward, because he went too far right, then left again. This will go on for several minutes while I'm patiently thinking he's bound to get it soon. All of a sudden he slams on the breaks, jumps out of the pickup and says calmly between clenched teeth, "It would help if you would tell me how far right or left I need to go."

O.K. I can do that. Just a couple of feet right, I say, now five feet left, no three feet right no back two and a half, now forward again. This time he jumps out of the pickup and rather than clenching his teeth he smiles so big his eyes disappear and I have to strain to make out his words. He says something like, "I think it would be more helpful if you stood over there," only he throws in a few more adjectives.

So I move to the side a few feet and politely ask, "over here?"

"No," he says. "Back farther... keep going... that's it ...a little more... just a little more. O.K. good."

By this time I'm 200 yards away, have waded through a creek and climbed over two fences. I yell, "Are you sure you can see me from clear over here?"

"Yeah, that's perfect," he shouts. "Now I don't have to kink my neck to see you."

What's even more disturbing than hand signals, though, is the difficulty in communicating when you're standing two feet away and talking directly to each other.

My husband came up to me and asked me the other day, "Can you saddle up your horse and go get a sick cow in?"

"Sure," I respond. "Where is she at?"

"She's in the north pasture," he says.

Now keep in mind I am one of those unfortunate souls who was born directionally challenged. So I ask, "Is that the one with the big red pipe?"

"Well, not exactly, it's near that field, but just a little west of it," he says.

"Oh," I say, thinking I understand. "You mean the one closest to the railroad tacks?"

"No," he says. "Down hill from that one."

Pondering this for a minute, I say, "Wouldn't that field actually be up hill?"

Then he looks at me with the big eye-hiding grin and pulls out a piece of paper from his pocket and quietly begins to draw a map. Immediately I understand.

"Well why didn't you say so. That's the one with the ditch curved like Mickey Mouse ears next to the railroad tracks by the wild rose bushes."

O.K, now that I have that settled, "Which cow is she?" I ask.

He says, "She's the brown one with the crooked neck."

I say, "Oh yeah, she has a white hip and a notch in her ear."

"No," he says. "That's a different one. This one is solid brown."

I ask, "Are you sure she's not more of a red color?"

"Ah, hell," he says. "I guess she's not even brown. In fact, come to think of it, she's not even sick."

There are times though that we communicate beautifully. I can be clear across the hay field repairing a different section of fence and my husband will hop up and down and flap his arms. To the untrained eye it may appear as if he wants me to fly like a goose with a broken wing, but I know from experience he just wants me to look at him.

Once he has my attention he will proceed through a series of carefully orchestrated movements. For instance, he will walk back and forth rapidly several times, squat on the ground with his arms extended as if he's lifting something heavy, turn his back side to me, slapping it; hit himself on the head and stagger around for minute, and walk back and forth again.

I know from these gracefully performed maneuvers he wants me to walk to the pickup, look in the back, get the sledge hammer and bring it to him.

Now that, I understand....

Ranch Wives Can't Jump

S ince I married a rancher and gave up my city life to move to the country 15 years ago, I've had to learn a lot of things about livestock, irrigating, farming, and ranchers in general. Things that someone who grew up on a ranch and takes for granted as being simple can be exceedingly difficult for the city slicker.

For instance, one of the hardest things I had to learn was how to jump off of a hay wagon, out of the back of a pickup bed, off of the back of 4-wheeler and from the cab of a tractor —all while in transit.

One might ask, "Why would you have to jump off while it's moving, couldn't you just stop?" And, of course, anyone who knows a rancher will answer that question with a resounding "noooooooooo!"

You see, ranchers can't stop, they can't even slow down because they always have to make good time, and their objective is to finish their chores faster than they did the day before — that's the real challenge in ranching — and most people think it's all about money.

And then there's the added benefit that if they can get their chores done quickly, when they meet the neighbors on the road they can say things like, "See that 400-acre field? I harrowed it in one day. Yessiree, the missus brought my lunch out on the four-wheeler and had the dog steer while she leaped onto the tractor like a flying circus act to deliver my sandwich. I didn't miss a beat, although the wife had a helluva time jumping back on the four-wheeler. The dog couldn't keep it straight — kept veering off looking at gophers...."

Anyway, if you haven't ever jumped off a moving vehicle, getting the hang of it is a little harder than it looks. The first time I jumped off the hay wagon when we were feeding cattle, I had to run ahead and open a gate so my husband wouldn't have to slow down and I figured that I darn sure better jump far enough away from the wagon that I didn't get run over by the back wheels. So I went to the far side of the wagon, got a run at it, and gracefully catapulted myself about 50 feet into the air and landed smack dab on my behind. If I had aimed a little better I could have cleared the fence and opened the gate from the other side. Needless to say, I couldn't sit down for a week.

On my second attempt, I followed the advice of a seasoned rancher who said to sit down on the very edge of the wagon and just stand up. I remember thinking that it couldn't be that simple, but who was I to question a rancher's wisdom? So I seated myself on the edge on the wagon, but before I had a chance to stand up, the wagon wheel hit a hole and I bounced off like a bag of groceries and once again landed on my backside.

Another well-meaning rancher told me to exit the wagon by stepping backwards off it. That way, he explained, I would be able to see exactly where I was in relation to the wagon and wouldn't have to worry about it. And he was absolutely right, I didn't have to worry about it because I could see the wagon coming and got a really close up view of it before it knocked me down.

Realizing that these ranchers meant well, and even followed up by watching from their places with binoculars, I finally decided I would just have to figure it out on my own. Besides, their wives were complaining that their husbands weren't getting much work done with all of the laughing and chortling going on.

So after several more attempts of jumping off at varying distances and speeds, performing knee tucks and nosedives with a half twist, I finally figured it out. The secret is to hit the ground running. I found that if I got my legs moving beforehand at approximately the same speed the wagon is moving and kept them going while jumping, I can hit the ground not only without falling, but I'm already running so it doesn't take as much effort to pass the tractor and make it to open the gate before he gets there.

Catching up to the wagon again after closing the gate takes an entirely different technique though. For several years I tried running and jumping onto the wagon. Sometimes I would make it and other times the only thing I could manage to get my hands on was the bundle of baling twine looped over a post on the wagon. I found that if I spread my feet out about shoulder width apart, I could hang on to the twine and surf across the pasture. Then when the wagon pulled me over a large enough cow pie, I could propel myself into the air with enough momentum to land on the wagon.

But I finally came across an easier way to get back on the wagon. In fact, it was so simple I don't know why I didn't think of it before. Once I jump off the wagon and run around and open the gate and close it behind the tractor, I simply stand with my arms folded across my chest and shoot him a look that says, "If you don't stop and let me back on the wagon you can feed the $$##!!!? cows yourself and while you're at it plan on making your own dinner and sleeping on the couch." Works every time....

Milk Comes From Cows, If You Know How To Get It

All cows are not created equal in ranchers' eyes. There are commercial cows, registered cows, young cows, old cows and all different breeds of cows, which you can pretty much group into one category.

And then there are milk cows....

Now, it's my understanding that all cows give milk, so I was perplexed to find out that while ranchers like cows, they tend to not be very fond of milk cows.

So when I mentioned to several ranchers, including my husband, Mike, of my desire to get a milk cow, most of them gave me that "look." It's the same kind of look you might get if your shopping cart accidentally plowed into their new pickup in the Safeway parking lot and left a small, but visible, dent. Somewhere between not very well concealed disappointment and confusion over your stupidity.

But I didn't want just any old milk cow, I explained. I wanted one with big brown eyes with long fluttery eyelashes and a cute face — like the "contented cow" on the Carnation evaporated milk can. Surely that should make a difference?

Mike tried to talk me out of it. "Wouldn't you rather have a nice new car," he says. "Or how about a Caribbean cruise, or I know, let's build on that family room you've been talking about."

But my mind was made up. "I want a milk cow," I insisted. (Visualize hands on hips, stomping feet here.)

So after several days of "discussing" my "Debra of Storybook Farms complex," he finally saw the error in his thinking (my mom always said I could argue a sharp pencil down to a nub) and agreed to help me find a cow.

We bought her from a dairy and it was love at first sight — my sight anyway. She was a Jersey with big brown eyes, fluttery lashes and the whole cute cow bit. She even had the perfect cute cow name — Bessie. Could it just get any better?

Around 6 a.m. the next morning, before he went to work, Mike gave me instructions on how to milk her, and found me a one-legged milk stool. After about 30 minutes of trying to figure out why it only had one leg and how to balance on it, I concluded that dairy companies must break the other three legs off to deter you from trying to milk a cow yourself and instead buy milk from them.

So after my stint of hopping around the barn on the stool like a kid on a pogo stick, I led Bessie in with a little grain and was ready to let the milking commence. Now, most people, myself included, realize that you don't just set the bucket under the cow and expect the milk to come pouring out, but what you might not realize is that there's more to it than just squeezing — I didn't anyway.

Consequently, I squeezed — nothing happened. I pulled — still nothing happened. I twisted — something happened — she kicked me square in the shin and knocked me off my one-legged stool.

Determined, I got back on the stool and tried again. This time, I remembered what Mike had said about using the thumb and index finger to start squeezing at the top before systematically squeezing with the other three fingers and managed to get some milk. I was so excited! I was actually milking a cow — not just any cow — my cow.

I looked up from the bucket to let out a whoop of triumph and Bessie smacked me right in the face with her wet tail (hopefully I don't have to explain to you why a cow's tail is almost always wet) and knocked me off my stool again.

But I persevered and two hours later, I had managed to get about a half-gallon of milk. The dairy said I could expect about one and a half gallons twice a day, so I knew it wasn't enough, but I decided that it wasn't bad for my first time.

So as I was admiring the creamy white liquid in awe of what I had just done and rubbing my hands, which were seemingly cramped permanently in the milking position, Bessie stuck her big dirty foot right in the bucket.

"I had plans for that milk," I shouted at her, but she didn't seem to care. Being optimistic by nature, I consoled myself with the fact that I could at least give it to the cats that had been meowing and circling the cow like vultures waiting for road kill ever since I brought her into the barn.

I tried to lift her foot out of the bucket to no avail. In fact, she shifted all of her weight to that single foot in the bucket, balancing herself similarly to my one legged milk stool. Not to be outdone by a cantankerous old Jersey, I put my backside against her hip that was supporting her, braced my feet on the barn wall and pushed with everything I had. It didn't even faze her. But she did turn, looked me square in the eyes with her big brown orbs and fluttery lashes, mooed a moo of disapproval and shuffled out the door with the bucket still on her foot.

Once she got outside she kicked if off, pausing for a moment to reflect upon the whole milking episode… then she stepped on the bucket, bending it so that one side was completely touching the other. It was no longer a round bucket, but a squashed piece of tin with a handle.

Then I got another one of those dent-in-the-pickup looks, but this time from the cats — like it was my fault they lost the milk that they shouldn't have been getting in the first place!

That night when Mike came in and asked me how the milking went, I tried to sound positive and said, "Great" as I dangled the wad of tin for him to see. Sensing that I was on the verge of tears and that laughing might get him in trouble, he offered to go help me with that night's milking. By then Bessie was so full she was practically squirting it out by herself and Mike got two and a half gallons of milk.

Gradually I learned how to milk and went from calling the cow "you flea-bitten bag of bones" back to her original name of Bessie. I also gained a better understanding of the difference between a "cow" and a "milk cow."

After several years, the excitement of getting up at the crack of dawn and making sure I was home every night by 6 p.m. to milk the cow finally wore off, so I bought three calves and told her to take care of them, which she readily did.

Now that the milk cow business is out of the way, I asked Mike about that Caribbean cruise. It's funny, he doesn't seem to recall anything about a cruise, a new car, or a family room. Go figure....

High-Centered On A
Fence Pole

I t was a beautiful day in the neighborhood, the sun
was shinning with nary a cloud in the brilliant blue
sky. The birds were singing, the squirrels were playing and I,
well… I was sort of stuck on the fence. High-centered, actually,
like a pickup with too low of a clearance.

It wasn't something I had planned, I didn't have it listed
as number three on my to-do list as in 1) Slop the hogs, 2) Feed
the chickens and 3) Watch husband laugh hysterically while I
hang by my armpits on the fence. No, it was completely
unintentional and executed obviously without any forethought
or afterthought, or really any kind of thought at all.

I had gone out with my husband, Mike, to help mend a
fence that the bulls had been rubbing against so hard that their
hides were permanently embossed with the swirling pattern of
fence pole bark. But then that's what bulls do to kill time in-
between escaping, trampling flower gardens and making
ranchers miserable.

But to give you an idea of what I was up against, the
fence is about six feet high and made of wood poles and posts.
The lower four feet on one side of the fence is covered with
woven wire, wire that is meshed together in such a way that it
forms rows of little squares. Squares, I discovered, that are too
small to get the toe of your shoe in.

Anyway, after performing my duties as Supply Acquisitions Person (SAP), which means I pack the poles needed to replace the broken ones, I was all set to help Mike.

He always performs the duties of The Power Tool Manager, or "The Man" for short, which basically means he gets to run the cordless power drill. I'm not sure why he gets to have the manager title for just running the drill, and I'm stuck being a SAP…. Well… O.K. — he does do a few other things like hewing out the poles, cutting them off, nailing them up, bending the wires, replacing the clips and assorted other tasks — but being the SAP is really hard work!

So after I laid out all of the poles needed along the length of the fence line, Mike asked me to "hop" over the fence and help him. Now, ordinarily I can climb over a fence with the best of them. After years of practice I've even found ways to topple over a fence without ripping my britches on the barbed wire. But I was on the side of the fence that had the woven wire attached and there were no footholds to climb up on.

Sensing my hesitation, Mike said, "It's easy, just get a run at it and hoist yourself up to the top pole and jump over."

"Okay, here goes," I said as I backed halfway across the field. I hunkered down like a racer on the starting block and took off. By the time I reached the fence I was at full speed, which for me is about the same as a slow jog for most people. I planted my feet and leaped into the air — all the while feeling that victory was mine — and landed on top of the fence pole hooked by my armpits.

Mike, still on the other side of the fence, "leisurely" rushed to my aid. He would have come faster but, as he noted later, it's hard to rush and laugh at the same time.

So there I was dangling like a kitten in a tree and the only thing Mike could think to do between holding his gut and wiping teary eyes was to grab my hands and pull. Well if you have ever had the misfortune of hanging by your armpits you'll know that the rest of your body doesn't easily follow your arms. It's like trying to pull over a bent pipe with a 100-pound weight attached to the other end. As Mike also later pointed out, the screaming in agony coming from me didn't help the situation much either.

So I summoned up all my strength, which isn't saying much, to try and hoist myself over as I tried to find a foothold. But my feet just kept peeling out on the slick wire as I dangled there helpless.

Apparently not knowing what else to do, Mike decided it would be appropriate to take this opportunity to show me how easily he can jump over the fence. He leaped from side to side doing one arm stands on the top pole and double flips over the fence as he said things like "See how easy it is," "That's all there is too it," "Piece of cake." To make matters worse, our Labrador, Puddin' Head, leaped around on the ground in unison with Mike. Together they looked like the Flying Schoeningh's Circus act. If I hadn't put an end to his nonsense by finally falling on my butt, Mike says he could have gone on for hours.

The only problem was that when I fell I was still on the wrong side of the fence. Not being one to make the same mistake twice, especially in front of The Man, I walked a little ways down the fence line to a pole that had broken and bent the wire up. I laid flat on the ground on my stomach and inched my way under the wire while fending off Puddin' Head's tongue that she was slopping all over my face.

When I got to my feet on the other side, trying to resume my dignity, I brushed off my pants and said, "O.K., now what was it you needed help with?" After getting no response I looked over and Mike was already on the opposite side of the fence heading for the pickup. He looked back over his shoulder and said, "Stop messing around and come back over the fence. It's time for lunch now, we'll finish this later this afternoon."

So I guess I've finally figured out why he's The Man and I'm the SAP.

E-mail — Spread It Around

I can remember a time when I couldn't wait to get on the Internet and become high-tech with correspondence. E-mail was just the neatest thing imaginable, being able to write notes and letters to anyone anywhere in the world.

I didn't stop to think that all the people I wanted to write to actually had to have computers and be on the Internet themselves. And ranchers aren't particularly known for having much enthusiasm over things that don't go moo or make money.

In fact, if you mention "high speed access," we ranchers hope someone has finally devised a way of jumping into the tractor faster and "broadband" Internet connections could mean that maybe there's something new on the market to replace baling twine.

Anyway, it's finally to the point that most of my ranching friends and family have Internet access. But now I'm not so sure I like e-mail. In the "old days" (the pre –computer era, which is something similar to the Paleozoic era in my son's eyes), I used to write a letter, stuff it into an addressed envelope, stamp it and throw it in the mailbox and then wait for a couple of weeks for a reply. Not too complicated, but it seemed to take way too long — or so I thought.

Now with the new "incredibly fast" e-mail system I just type a letter and click "send," and sometimes wait only a matter of minutes or hours for a reply. But here's the catch, and you know there's always a catch. When I get a reply, I have to sift through 500 other e-mails in my inbox to find it. It's like trying to sort a renegade heifer out of the neighbor's 500-cow herd.

And the e-mails are all "junk mail." None of them even have anything to do with cows or ranching. One hundred out of every 500 e-mails are advertisements for Viagra. What in the world is a rancher going to do with Viagra? We don't have enough time to get the chores done as it is.

Several of the e-mails say something to the effect of "Get the loan you need, today!" Obviously they don't know they are e-mailing a rancher because if very many of us took them up on their offer, they would go broke. After all, what rancher doesn't need a loan today?

Then there are the "Work At Home" e-mail ads. What do they think ranchers do? They act like this is some kind of new concept they are presenting.

Some e-mail advertisers do have a sense of humor though. I usually get about five e-mails every day that say "Get Out of Debt Fast!!!" Like a rancher could really ever get out of debt, jeesh!

Once in awhile I get an e-mail that promises to get rid of "worm viruses," but unfortunately I haven't been able to get Norton Antivirus software uploaded to my dogs yet — they don't give very good instructions on where to put it and the dogs don't seem to tolerate my trying very well.

"Free Cell Phone" e-mails are always interesting. Sure, you get the phone for free — all you have to do is pay $50 a month to use it and donate half your kidney.

This one always gets me, "Do you have heartburn?" Apparently these people have never seen the empty bottles of Extra Strength Mylanta rolling around on the floorboards of rancher's pickups, in the cabs of their tractors or lined up along their barn walls. What rancher doesn't have heartburn?

I really like the one that says, "Meet Singles In Your Area." First of all, how do they even know where my area is? And second, if I wanted to meet singles I wouldn't meet them in my area where everyone would find out.

I couldn't even begin to tell you how many "Fabulous Vacation Cruises" I've won. They will pay for my "luxurious state room," I just have to find a way to be flown by private jet out to where the ship is currently located somewhere in the middle of the Caribbean and be parachuted on board inside of a crate marked "Perishable Food Items."

I got one today that said, "Tired Of Looking Like A Hairy Gorilla?" How did they know? I tell you these people are amazing....

I'm sure a lot of people can appreciate the e-mails that say, "No Prescription Required — Cheap Drugs." Do they think that we will actually order "cheap" drugs from them when we can go stand on any street corner and find them without having to pay postage?

One of my favorites is the e-mail that I have been seeing a lot lately that reads, "Free Smiley Faces For Your E-Mail." You open it up and it says something to the effect that now you can customize all of your e-mails with more than 100 different "smiley faces." They have smiley faces winking, blinking and nodding. Some are laughing, some are crying and others have braces. But I have yet to see one that conveys the message I'm looking for — "I'm replying to this e-mail to inform you that unsolicited advertisements will be turned over to our Pasture Manager who will place them in a manure spreader for proper handling."

When Iris Eyes Are Smiling

I magine a sea of pink and white petunias springing from the soil like nature's art, full of vibrant colors and velvety textures perfectly painted against a background of Shasta daisies swaying in the gentle breeze. Behind the daisies a rock wall provides support to the magnificent towering irises with a combination of lavender, white, blue and yellow bearded petals reaching up to luminous skies of blue.

Then picture Puddin' Head, a black Labrador/Lord-only-knows-what retriever, playfully romping through the flower garden plucking up the $3 a bulb irises one by one before they've even had an opportunity to reach the desired state described above, and carrying them off to unknown destinations.

Then add a rancher's wife to the scene, running through the barnyard in the early morning hours in a robe and pink fuzzy slippers chasing a black dog, twirling a bag of bagels overhead like a cowboy with a lasso (the only weapon at her disposal at the time) while her husband, Mike, calls after her from the open house door, "What about breakfast?"

I planted the expensive irises between some other irises that a neighbor had given me for free and Puddin' Head, being a discriminating horticulturist, carefully picked through and selected the expensive ones for this particular adventure.

When I finally caught up with her she spat out the "China Dragon," "Swing Town" and "Engaging Blue" iris varieties preferring the "Home Style" bagels that I had pelted her with.

Although somewhat worse for wear and slobbered on, the irises appeared to be salvageable, unlike my fuzzy slippers that had not survived the trek through the cattle pens unsoiled. I replanted the irises and this time covered them with wire mesh to discourage Puddin' from attempting a repeat of her bulb raid. My carefully planned garden — complete with a map showing where each variety was planted — was no longer neatly in order, but at least the bulbs were back in the ground.

Having taken care of that, I went back in for breakfast, which my husband, not knowing how long my pursuit would last, had finished cooking. Taking advantage of my absence, he slightly rearranged my healthy menu of bagels (which were no longer an option anyway) and fruit, and presented a breakfast of potatoes and eggs slathered in a pound of bacon grease.

Not wanting to disappoint the cook, as he was obviously pleased with his presentation, I sat down to eat the cholesterol-elevating plate of lard, when Mike said with a mischievous grin, "Someone's looking at you."

Sure enough, Puddin' was standing at the sliding glass doors with a mouth full of irises wagging her tail and smiling at me with shining eyes. Sensing my irritation from the string of adjectives that came out of my mouth, Mike, who has been trying to train her to hunt ducks, said I needed to reward her for retrieving. I said, "Why, in case we decide to go iris hunting some day?"

But taking this into consideration, I opened the door and Puddin' came in and dutifully dropped the irises at my feet and sat as Mike had taught her waiting for an encouraging word and a tasty tidbit.

"Well," said my husband, "Give her something to show her what a good dog she is for bringing them to you."

I glanced at my plate of floating grease gravy sitting on the table, but before I could take any longer to consider that possibility, Mike jumped up and said, "You can't feed a dog that junk!"

So he went and got Puddin' a dog biscuit and motioned for me to sit down and eat the "wonderful breakfast that he had cooked for me." Now I may not be the sharpest tool in the shed, but something seemed amiss. Why is it "junk" for her and "wonderful" for me?

But when I sat down and begrudgingly took a bite, the wonderful flavor of long-missed bacon grease hit my taste buds and I no longer cared whether or not it was "junk." I just savored the moment and thanked Puddin' for the iris adventure that led me to a morning of mouth-watering bliss.

'Anyone Can Do It...'

When I married my rancher husband, Mike, 16 years ago, no one told me that there was some kind of unwritten law that the wife always takes over the bookkeeping duties. Of course, he was the one who told me that, and even though I haven't been able to verify it, I know it must be true — because a lot of other ranch wives seem to be in the same predicament.

The chore itself isn't too bad, but I decided that more than a decade of bookkeeping without a comfortable desk was enough. When I informed Mike of my decision to approach my wifely ranching duties from a more professional standpoint and buy a desk, he was a little surprised.

"I thought you liked using the living room floor," he said.

Ignoring his blatant attempt at trying to get me to save money, I headed for the nearest office supply store. Hoping that no one saw me stagger in surprise at the cost, I slowly moved through the rows of desks. I passed by the cherry and maple and went on to the pine and finally way back in a dimly lit corner, I found my little gem — 100 percent particle board with wood-look veneer, $149.99 — today only.

When I told the clerk of my selection she called someone from the storeroom to bring it out. A few minutes later a young man came wheeling out a large flat box on a dolly. "Here you go ma'am," he said.

Puzzled by his offer, I said, "Oh no, that must be for someone else. I'm waiting for a desk." The adolescent smacked his gum loudly and gave an irritated sigh, "This is it. It's in the box in a bunch of pieces," he said.

Even more confused, I looked at the female clerk for some sign of help, "He's right, this is your desk," she said. "You just have to put it together."

Undaunted by another one of my staggers of surprise, she continued to ring it up. "Don't worry," she said. "See, it says right on the box, 'So easy, anyone can do it.' "

"But that looks like someone wrote it on the box with a black marking pen," I protested. "Are you sure it's that easy"?

"Oh that's just some creative advertising from the company," she said. "Sort of catches your eye doesn't it, hon? That'll be $149.99."

It was then it dawned on me that all store clerks call middle-aged ranching wives "hon" for some reason. I made a mental note to dwell on that later as I shoveled out the cash, all the while mentally cheering myself on with the "anyone can do it" phrase.

Ranchers are a trusting lot. We believe the experts when they say the cattle prices will rise, the drought is over and buying emus and llamas is a good investment. So why wouldn't I believe this nice woman when she said anyone can do it?

Eager to get started, I took my new prize home and scattered its contents on the living room floor along with the 400-page assembly novel.

Ignoring the fine print that said "may need a table saw and a wood planer if the pieces don't fit properly," I gathered the needed supplies —hammer, screwdriver and my purple glue stick.

After 4 1/2 hours of working on the desk, two of which were spent reading the instructions, I became convinced that the phrase "anyone can do it" was a cruel revenge written on the box by some disgruntled store employee who was forced to put together 15 display desks — more than likely someone who really couldn't do it.

But persistence paid off and two days later, I stood back and looked at my creation with the sense of pride that comes from almost doing a job well. It was a little misshapen and not quite level, but it was finally done.

I grabbed a chair, sat down at my new desk and rested my elbows on the top as I mulled over where to place my supplies. My contentment didn't last long — 30 seconds later the desk crashed to the floor.

As I lay there on the floor under a heap of particleboard, laminate and wet purple glue, Mike walked in. He has an uncanny way of showing up at the most inopportune times. He examined the situation for a brief moment and said, "So I see you decided the floor was the best place after all."

When his fits of convulsive laughter finally subsided three days later, he offered to help. First I was informed that a kitchen knife is not the same thing as a flathead screwdriver and the butt end of a meat cleaver won't pass as a hammer.

And most importantly, it has to be Elmer's Wood Glue. He explained that any rancher caught using anything other than Elmer's Wood Glue is immediately kicked out of the sacred circle of manly ranchmen. He said the only thing worse is actually doing the things on their wife's Honey-do list.

Under his skillful hands it finally took shape and became the solid desk it was meant to be — for anyone with a shop full of power tools, that is.

But it was worth all the effort because now when the neighbors stop by and marvel at how nice it looks and ask if it was hard to put together, I just smile and say, "Not at all, anyone can do it."

Belly Surfing With Draft Horses

D raft horses have been used for more than a century to work the fields and to do everything from pulling stumps to raking hay. But few are aware of their ability to provide rides that would rival those of southern California amusement parks.

Our first experience with these "gentle giants" began when my husband, Mike, came walking down the driveway leading two Belgian draft horses behind him like a kid with his new puppies. The huge smile of satisfaction on his face was dampened only by the look of disbelief on mine.

"Aren't they cute?" he asks. I don't know if you could actually describe 2,500-pound animals that are six feet tall at the withers with hooves the size of dinner plates as "cute." But I was willing to give it a try.

He said we really "needed" them to pull our cattle feed-wagon, and although they were well broke, there would be a "brief" training period to get them accustomed to the cattle.

And so the experience began. Mike built a training sled that was heavy enough that most horses would have had a difficult time pulling it, but these weren't most horses. To give you an idea of how the events transpired, we started off calling them their given names, "Bob" and "Doc" but as time wore on we developed other names for them that aren't suitable for publication, but needless to say, better described their personalities.

Mike was so excited the first day he decided to take them out for a test run, that he asked his dad, Pete, to go along for the ride. Pete has always been a sensible person, so it's hard to say exactly why he threw caution to the wind on this particular day and decided to join Mike. Having been partly responsible for feeding and harnessing the animals during the previous weeks, I got a close up view of just how strong and large they were and quickly, but graciously, declined the ride — I said, "No way."

Pete stepped onto the training sled and, trying to be supportive of his son's ranching project, noted that the horses looked very calm and relaxed. Mike was all smiles, as he proudly said, "Aren't they great, I just can't believe I was able to find this nice of horses around here."

Pete said, "Yeah, that's terrific Mike," as he sat down on the hay bale, which was strapped to the wagon to use as a seat. "But how do you make theses things go?" And as it turned out "go" was the magic word. Upon hearing it, Bob and Doc twitched their ears, and shifted their weight to their hind legs as they reared up slightly and took off from a seeming idle position to a full gallop. It reminded me of a Maserati going from 0 to 60 in less than 10 seconds.

Pete fell over backward and promptly rolled off the sled within the first minute of the ride. He staggered back to the barn while holding his back and muttering under his breath — not unlike the Yosemite Sam cartoon character. This was his first and final experience with the draft horses.

Pete and I watched in amazement as the horses continued to drag the sled with Mike still on it at warp speeds through the maze of corrals. Mike struggled to gain control by forcing them into a tight circle. The only problem was that the horses kept up the same speed and the sled was almost flying sideways around the circle. By this time the gravitational force was pulling Mike's face back to his hairline, which made it look like he was smiling — really big.

The fiasco finally ended about an hour later when the horses had nowhere to go but head on into a fence. They slid to an abrupt stop, noses almost touching the top fence rail, doing the reverse — 60 to 0 in less than 10 seconds. The force from the unexpected stop catapulted Mike off the wagon and onto the ground. Of course, he later said he purposely planned on leaping ten feet into the air, clearing the horses backs and landing near their heads so he could grab them quickly — the flip with a half twist, landing face first, was an afterthought.

I've heard that you can learn from others' mistakes, but I must have not been very receptive to that bit of wisdom. Several weeks later after the first snowfall Mike said, "I've got them figured out now, let's hook Bob and Doc up to the hay wagon and feed with them this morning," and I actually agreed to do it and without the promise of so much as a night out on the town. I missed my opportunity for what I later found out would have been a well-deserved bribe.

Everything was going smoothly, Mike was driving the team and I was on the back of the wagon flaking off baled hay and feeding it to the cattle. It was peaceful without the deafening roar of the tractor that we usually fed with. It reminded me a little of "dashing through the snow in a two-horse hay wagon."

It didn't last long. One of the yearling calves was feeling so good he took off running and bucking and in the process he was loudly releasing a little methane gas into the ozone layer. Having little exposure to cattle in the first place and certainly never having had the opportunity to hear their unmannerly bodily functions, the horses were scared — and off they went.

The faster the horses ran, the faster the calves chased the wagon that held their breakfast. While Mike was trying to control the runaway horses, I was on the back of the wagon cramming my fingers between the floorboards trying to find a place to hang on.

When it became apparent that I couldn't hold on any longer, I jumped off and landed with my right foot in a gopher hole, twisting my ankle. It wouldn't have been too bad but I also landed right in front of 500 yearling calves that were running right at me in their quest for food. I managed to half crawl and walk to the side of the field, narrowly escaping the trampling hooves.

In the meantime, the horses hit a big hole, which spilled several bales of hay onto the ground for the calves, so they stopped chasing the wagon. But in the process the horses had broken free of the wagon and, Mike not being one to give up easily, was still hanging onto the reins. At this point with no wagon holding them back, the horses were able to increase their speed, which they readily did every time they looked back and saw Mike belly surfing through the snow behind them as he maintained his grip on the reins.

Once in awhile they would slow down enough that Mike could get on his knees, and one time he almost made it to his feet before they looked back and got scared again. Since there wasn't any way I could help, and he was ignoring my pleas for him to let go of the reins, I began judging his snow surfing abilities. I think he could have won something for his one handed roll over with a knee to the chin if this had been an actual competition.

The horses zigzagged across the field for a good 20 minutes before screeching to a halt in a fenced corner of the field. Mike stood up, dug the snow out of his coat and pants and led them back to the barn. This is actually when Bob and Doc began to develop their new names. I suspect he was having a difficult time deciding on which of the long list of names to use that he had given them during his snow-surfing demonstration. In the end, he used them all — several times.

You would think that would be the end of it, but he talked me into feeding with them several times after that — determined to make it work, and it did — occasionally. But we (mainly me) finally tired of the daily race around the field and eventually sold them to a man who uses them in draft horse pulling competitions. Which, by the way, we found out later was what they were originally trained for — and I hear they are doing quite well.

The Social Status Of Cows

I f you watch cows long enough you will discover that they have distinct personalities, much like humans. In fact, being herd oriented, they even form their own little cliques. In other areas of the world I'm sure cows have banded together to form all types of groups within their bovine societies, but these are some of the social orders that we have found in our own cattle.

Valley Girl Cows — These cows walk around prim and proper, fluttering their eyelashes. When standing, they always have one hip cocked to the side and have a like totally "meaux" attitude. Most of these cows were imports from California; however, a few locally raised cows have adopted the Valley Girl mind set.

Home Girl Cows — These cows walk through the herd with an extra spring in the step and an exaggerated jiggle in the udders. They spend their days chilling with their peeps. Come to think of it, that's how they spend their nights too. When fed hay they act indifferent as if to say, "Yo, wud up wit dis? That stuff's so played out, keep it outta my grill (face). That rancher's whack!"

Nerd Cows — Nerd cows are a little on the thin side. They hitch their tails up high and have an exaggerated cowlick on top of their heads that sticks out like a third horn. And instead of saying moo they say "muh (duh)." You'll often find nerd cows peeking through your windows watching as you work on your computer.

Athletic Cows or Female Jocks — These cows are easy to spot. They have more muscling than the average cow and consequently walk with a wider stance and a turned in shoulder. They are always competing with each other having field races and broad jumps while discreetly trying to figure out ways to pole vault over the fence. Many of the more muscled cows have aspirations of running for governor of California.

Type A Cows — Cows with Type A personalities are always the first ones to push their way to the water trough. They often experience "Trail Rage" when someone cuts in front of them and can be seen butting heads with other cows at the slightest provocation.

Fence Walkers — Fence Walkers are always strutting along the fence lines enticing the neighbor's bulls with phrases like "Hey big boy, why don't you jump over and see me some time." Many Fence Walkers spent their younger heifer years in Nevada and learned the trait from their mothers, commonly referred to as Madams.

Cows From The Wrong Side Of Tracks — These cows are harder to spot in a herd because no one knows for sure what side is the wrong side of the tracks.

In Search Of The Elusive Tamarack

W hen we converted our two wood stoves to propane a couple of years ago I thought my wood cutting days were over – no more mess, no more splinters, no more work and no more searching for the perfect tree. In fact I was so excited I did my hallelujah dance. Well actually it's more of a shuffle than a dance...well O.K.... I just sat in a chair, raised my arms and said woohoo! But you get the point; it was a pretty exciting moment.

But alas, as fate would have it, or rather my husband, Mike, would have it, we once again own a wood-burning unit. To be honest, I could probably live without the stove, but Mike says it's the single most important element in "our" lives right now and getting wood for it is nearly a life or death situation because the stove is situated in the hub of our very existence – the place where "it" (I haven't quite figured out what "it" is yet) all happens — his shop.

A rancher's shop is like his sanctuary and next to his power tools, a wood stove that allows you to work in comfort during the winter, is pretty much like the Holy Grail. So you can see how important it is to spend every waking second either scouting the hillsides looking for wood or at least thinking about where you might go to find it.

But it can't be just any kind of wood — even though it has been my experience that any kind of wood burns — it has to be tamarack.

Finding a tamarack when you want one is like trying to find a buck during deer season — they're just nowhere around. Since tamaracks don't have legs, I'm convinced that they bend and duck behind a pine tree when they see you coming.

We probably could have found more of them if it wasn't for not being able to get off of the main road and actually get into the forest, presumably where the trees are. Every time we came to a Forest Service road I would yell, "There's a road, let's go get that tamarack and go home."

So Mike would drive up the road as I excitedly scouted the area for tamaracks and inevitably about 200 yards later we'd run into a big mound of dirt closing the road. And the roads were never closed at the beginning of the road, that would be too easy; instead they pile the dirt up just far enough down the road that you can't see it until it's too late. Two hours and 30 blocked roads later, I started to lose what little enthusiasm that I had mustered up for this adventure.

At about that time Puddin' Head our black lab and official woodcutting dog who sat next to me in the pickup stopped sticking her tongue in my ear and slobbering all over me, and laid down. When she stops being excited, you know it's getting bad.

As we drove around aimlessly on closed roads, I tried to point out to Mike that during a forest fire all of the trees are burned, including the abundant pine, fir and spruce, not just the tamarack. So I told him that I'm pretty sure that they are capable of igniting and burning in a wood stove as well. I even went so far as to suggest that I saw an ad in the newspaper about firewood for sale.

He immediately gave me that look, the look that says, "How dare you even think that I could put just any old pine tree in my shop stove!" Apparently I had lost my senses for a moment and had forgotten the significance of this little outing, we weren't getting wood for just a stove, but "the" stove.

Desperate to find a tamarack so we could get this over with and go home, I started looking on the down side of the hill next to the road... where lo and behold there laid the biggest tamarack I had ever seen. It had apparently fallen over in a storm and had gone unnoticed by previous woodcutters.

"Stop!" I yelled. "There's a big honking tamarack down there."

Mike slammed on the brakes and after a couple of seconds of careful consideration said, "Yeah, right, I bet it's just another pine tree — you're not going to trick me this time."

"No honest," I insisted, "it's a huge tamarack just laying down there on the ground."

He finally got out and looked, and surmised that I was correct, and yes indeed it was a tamarack. Actually I had no idea what kind of tree it was when I yelled, but I figured it was big and that in itself might be enough to entice him so we could go home and I could get on with more important things.

There was only one problem —the tree lay at the bottom of a steep 30-foot embankment in a little dip, and below that was an even steeper hillside that dropped down into a raging river.

"Oh well, too bad," I said. "Guess we'll have to look for something a little easier."

But it was too late. He had already gotten out the chainsaw and the woodcutting light was dancing in his eyes.

"Look," he said. "I'll trim the branches and stomp the ground down a little and make a path for you. If you walk sideways at an angle you should be able to make it up the hill with the wood."

It sounded like a good plan and like a sap I fell for it — literally. I took one step down the bank, tripped over a root and fell halfway down the hillside.

"Stop messing around, we have work to do," Mike yelled over his shoulder as he cut the first piece, which immediately rolled down the hill and into the river.

He then decided that I would have to catch the pieces as he cut them to keep them from rolling and then pack them up the hill to the truck. This worked pretty well for awhile until he got about 15 feet down the 100-foot long tree from the top and the width of the pieces started to increase.

I tried packing a few of them up the bank and ended up on my knees rolling them up the hill like human bulldozer with our faithful dog, not one to miss an opportunity when someone has their hands occupied, began running beside me licking my face and nipping at my heels.

"This just isn't going to work," I protested.

"Sure it is, we can't give up now," said Mike. "Go get me the ax."

So after he cut the pieces and I saved them from rolling down the hill, he split them into two pieces so I could get them up the bank. As Mike worked his way down the tree the pieces continued to increase in size and pretty soon he was having to split them two or three times.

Finally, after about four hours of this routine and as it was nearing dark, we managed to get a truckload.

Like hunters bagging the big one, we were on an adrenaline high all the way home excitedly talking about how we managed to get such a nice big tree, and not just any tree, but the prized tamarack.

I couldn't believe I had balked at the thought of woodcutting again, I told Mike. I said it was so much fun to get out and work this hard and bring home a trophy for all our efforts, it really makes a person feel good. We even made plans to go back the following day and get the rest of the tree.

Once we got home though, it took another hour to unload the monster load of firewood and by the time we showered, ate and got to bed it was almost 11 p.m. We lay in bed for a few moments reminiscing about the day's event, but it took on a decidedly different tone than our previous woodcutting high.

I complained about my back pain. Mike complained about his arms and shoulders hurting from all the wood splitting. I said my legs were already getting sore from all that walking up the hill. Mike said his feet hurt from standing all day. I said my face and ears were chapped from Puddin' licking them so much.

About the time I was trying to figure out how in the world I was going to get out of going after the rest of that tree the next morning, especially after my little spiel about how good it felt to work that hard, Mike turned to me and said, "I bet pine would burn just as well as tamarack, where did you say you saw that ad for firewood for sale?"

War Of The Weeds

A s all good things must end the peaceful existence I had with my lawn during the winter months of white fluff came to a screeching halt when the grass turned green and started to grow this spring. Not that I have a problem with this growing carpet of sod.....it's what happened next.

I awoke the other morning and as my usual routine dictates I looked out the window to watch the rising sun. As it came over the mountains and slowly worked its way across the yard revealing the lush green lawn, I noticed something was different. I expected to see a smooth flat sea of green from mowing the lawn the day before. What I saw were little dark clumps that appeared to be strategically placed throughout the yard. I got out my binoculars for a closer look and there they were, like aliens from outer space, trying to take over the grass — DANDELIONS.

It has been said in order to effectively fight your enemy, get to know your enemy. With no time to lose I ran to the bookcase and opened up a book on tactical war maneuvers, cleverly disguised as a botanical book on native plants. I learned that Georg Heinrich Weber, a German professor, first classified the dandelion that was brought to the New World by European settlers. And they brought it deliberately!

We can't blame our forefathers for this terrible travesty because the book said the Taraxacum Officinale better known as the Dandelion, Pissabed (because of its diuretic properties), Priest's Crown and Telltime, claimed to be a member of the Composite Family and presented itself as a medicinal plant. The Mohegans and other Indians drank tea made from the leaves and roots to cure ailments, and settlers later introduced it to the Midwest because of its long blooming season to provide food for the bees.

It's hard to say when this seemingly benign plant turned on us and became our enemy, although I'm suspecting it may have had something to do with its ability to change form and become an intoxicating liquor known as dandelion wine.

Equipped with this knowledge — and territorial by nature — I knew there was little time. If the dandelions are allowed to mature they will turn in to downy white balls and begin their raid from the air. I ran to the garage, still in my flannel nightgown, and surveyed my arsenal.

Knowing the crafty nature of this creature, I decided on a high-powered spray gun attached to an oversized tank of an unknown chemical agent that had been in our garage so long no one remembered what it was. I strapped the contraption to my back and outfitted myself with protective goggles and a gas mask for excessive spray (no sense taking any chances). As a last show of force I attached lawn aerator sandals to my pink fuzzy slippers. I figured not only would they intimidate the enemy, I might as well do some good while I'm out there.

Ready for combat, I stepped onto the lawn like Neil Armstrong beginning his lunar walk.

The dandelions proved to be a worthy adversary. They grew together in clumps circling like wagon trains in a John Wayne movie, protecting the women and children. Their bright yellow flowers would tilt providing an armored shield, reflecting the sun and temporarily blinding me as I spun about dazed and confused spraying everything in sight.

What's worse, my pink fuzzy slippers were covered with yellow stains no doubt attributed to the dandelion's paint bombing abilities. It seemed as though every time I neutralized one of the self-pollinating creatures, it would produce three more to take its place.

At one point my husband yelled from the porch, "Watch out there's one coming at your hind leg." (I made a mental note to get him away from the cattle occasionally.) I quickly whirled around tangling my aerator sandals together and managed to maintain my balance for a split second before falling into an undignified flannel heap on the ground.

Now eyeball to eyeball with the archenemy we carefully scrutinized each other. Poised with my finger on the trigger I took deadly aim with my high-powered weapon and my hand began to tremble. I realized for a brief instant, it's true what they say, never look into the eyes of the enemy or you will loose your ability to shoot him. I dropped my gun and I thought I saw him sigh with relief although it could have been the wind blowing.

Memories began to flood my mind of childhood days when someone would pluck a dandelion and rub it on my chin to see if I liked boys. Although the outcome isn't important at this time, I do believe it's a ritual still practiced today.

And I remembered all of the times my once young son would bring me a dandelion bouquet. Proud of his accomplishment I would put them in a vase setting them on the dinning room table for all to admire.

It was right then and there I decided to cease and desist all aggressive action against this Priest's Crown, the Telltime, this Pissabed if you will. This once noxious weed suddenly turned into a delicate little flower right before my eyes. As I scanned over the sea of green laced with yellow flowers, I started questioning my previous animosity toward these alien creatures. Peace negotiations began and we reached an amicable agreement — as long as they don't try to completely take over, they can stay.

Although I do lop one's head off with the lawn mower from time to time, I no longer consider the dandelion an archenemy. I am currently devoting my time and energy to the annihilation of another well-known adversary, the Thistle. Once again in referencing my tactical war maneuvers book I find its real name is Cnicus Benedictus. Just as I suspected, a direct descendant of Benedict Arnold, all the time befriending you with its pretty purple flowers and then sticking you when and where you least expect it. The war rages on....

'Bubba' The Calf

C alving season has always been one of the most enjoyable times of the year for me, and not just because my husband, Mike does all of the work. Every year I look forward to having at least one bottle baby and I've never been disappointed.

There's always the young heifer that won't take her calf or the cow that has twins and doesn't have enough milk for two. Once the newborn accepts you as their human parent, they are generally a pleasure to be around. I've always been grateful for this yearly opportunity to raise God's little creatures. Until last year...

His name was Bubba. It was a difficult birth, not for him but for his mother. She was a good cow, still is, but as fate would have it she gave birth to a 105 pound bouncing baby boy. Keeping in mind the average calf weighs around 75 pounds, you can imagine her bewilderment when the stork showed up with this one. As soon as the calf hit the ground he was up and running. Unfortunately, so was the mother — she took one look at Bubba and ran for her life.

Mike tried to go after her to reunite the cow with her precious bundle of joy, thinking surely it was some kind of postpartum phenomenon that could be quickly resolved. As it turns out, it was postpartum fear. She hurdled two fences like an Olympic champion and headed into the next county.

I told Mike not to worry, raising orphaned calves has become my specialty. Thrilled at the first opportunity of the year to bottle feed a calf, I ran to the house to mix the formula. Moments later Mike came in and said in an unusually melodic voice, "The little guy's waiting for you in the barn."

Although Mike's smile was larger than normal and a little bit devious, I didn't really think much about it at the time. I had become accustomed to the half-crazed look that most ranchers wear during calving season due to sleep deprivation. Just the night before I had found him aimlessly wandering around the house at 2 a.m. running into walls like he was on some kind of bumper car amusement ride.

So I began the usual routine, which consisted of a four-hour ordeal of cornering the frightened calf, forcing the bottle in his mouth and trying to teach him to suck on something that must taste and feel like a used tire.

The first two days were typical of how most calves respond so it wasn't until later that I realized the reason for Mike's covert source of amusement. By the third day Bubba had developed a voracious appetite. He knew I was the one with the food and he was going to get as much as he could even if he had to use force. I walked in as usual, closed the door and turned to face him. Bubba ran at me like a bull in a Spanish arena after a red cape.

He knocked me off of my feet and the bottle went flying. He chased the bottle around the barn floor with his nose until he finally realized the bottle was useless without me to hold it.

I had just regained my balance and what was left of my dignity when he came after me again. As he searched for food he began butting my legs with enough intensity that he managed to knock me down a few more times. The ungraceful manner in which the calf catapulted me around the barn left me staggering like the loser on Saturday Night Wrestling. Up until now I had only witnessed this kind of entertainment. I now had the privilege of participating.

By the time I finally got the bottle in his mouth he drank all of the milk down like there was no tomorrow. But Bubba wanted more and he wanted it now.

In an effort to subdue him, I tried a tactic I'd often seen at rodeos in the bulldogging event. I grabbed him around the neck and wrestled him to the ground and promptly sat on him.

Before I had a chance to say, "Take that, you ungracious bovine," Bubba somehow managed to fling me face first on the floor. As he stood over me looking like a poster calf for "Got More Milk?" I sensed there was a feeling of superiority coming from him.

Although somewhat unsuccessful, my tackle, or his, depending on which way you want to look at it, seemed to calm him a little. I thought the battle was over and as I turned to leave, I seemed to remember a saying about never turning your back on the enemy coming to mind, but for some reason it didn't register at the time.

Unfortunately, Bubba wasn't ready to give up. He gathered up some speed for this one and planted his rock hard head firmly on my backside. He got my attention, but not the milk he was looking for—-I made a run for the door. He blocked my every move, when I zigged he counter zagged. Finally I threw the empty bottle across the floor and when he dove after it I made my escape.

Daily food fights with Bubba became an unpleasant ritual four times a day, which began to take its toll. I became, well...let's say mildly annoyed at every new bruise I acquired. I not so lovingly referred to Bubba as the mammoth calf from down under, and I didn't mean Australia.

A short time later a cow had a calf that didn't survive and while Mike was pondering whether or not to try and get her to adopt Bubba, I shoved them into a pen together. I wasn't about to feed this guy any longer than I had to.

The cow was leery of Bubba at first, probably thinking the week-old calf was big enough to be weaned by now. After running in circles trying to get away from him, she finally gave in to Bubba's persistence. Bubba would nurse with such enthusiasm he would literally lift the cow's hind legs off the ground. I suspect she wanted a calf pretty bad, and I wasn't about to convince her otherwise.

This year I gave all of the cows a lecture and told them, "You're the ones who wanted to have a calf in the first place. That makes them your responsibility and you'll have to feed and take care of them yourselves." So far they've listened, but I used the same kind of psychology on Mike when he bought the cows, and you can see how that turned out.

Baling Twine 101

When I married into the ranching industry, one of my first lessons was in baling twine protocol. You might think that baling twine is just something to hold hay together in a bale, and it is, but baling twine is also the cornerstone of all ranching activities.

Without it, how would ranchers hold fences together? What else would they tie their stock dogs up with when they won't stop chasing the neighbor's cattle? They wouldn't be able to keep the bumper on that old Ford truck without baling twine. And some wouldn't be able to shut a gate, close a door or keep a tractor hood secured in the down position without baling twine.

As you can see, it has a multitude of uses, so it is essential to learn the proper handling of baling twine, and that knowledge has been handed down from generation to generation since the days of yore.

History books have revealed that some form of baling twine was used as early as the 1800s. One notable passage was from the book, "Feeding the Cows," written in 1829 by Maken Nomoney, where a farmer reprimanded his son by saying "You pulleth those trousers up with thine bailing twine boy."

Now that I think about it ranchers might be able to make some extra cash by selling baling twine to the plumbing industry for that same use.

The first thing that I learned about baling twine was that it has to be organized — you can't just wad the stuff up and throw it in a big heap — it has to be neatly tied and then thrown in a big heap. You may find yourself wondering why this makes a difference since it all ends up in a pile anyway, but trust me; there is nothing that will get you in more trouble with a rancher than messing with his twine system.

First of all, you have to get the twine off of the bale and there are several things to consider — which side of the bale to cut, where on the twine to make the cut and what implement to cut it with. For this discussion we will consider small two string bales. Trying these techniques with large three and six string bales could cause even more hernias, ruptured discs and greater malaise than you get with the smaller bales.

Most ranchers use pocketknives or a used sickle blade from a swather, which has been transformed into a cutting tool. However, it is seldom that ranch wives are allowed to use these manly devices so a kitchen steak knife will suffice. (Helpful Hint: Ranchers will usually allow you to use their sharp shovel to cut the twine, but only if you promise to dig a couple of postholes with it when you are done.)

Once you have selected a cutting tool, the bales must be rotated so that the knots tied by the baling machine are on top of the bale. Now for the incision, the twine must be cut exactly 1/2 inch in front of the knot. Cutting too close to the knot or too far from the knot could cause the demise of the ranching industry as we know it. (Helpful Hint: I got this one from Martha Stewart — Tape a small laminated paper ruler to the side of your steak knife handle — It's a good thing!)

While hand feeding cattle from the back of a hay wagon, you must learn to juggle several cut strands of twine at once. This is because you are not allowed to put a strand down at anytime during the feeding process. I'm not sure why this is, but I found that doing so causes a rancher to swear, flail his arms and dart around the hay wagon like a chicken with a fox in the henhouse.

On a similar note, you can't tie a few strands together or tie even half of the strands together, you must keep them neatly organized until you are completely finished, whether you have 10 bales with 20 strings or 40 bales with 80 strings, it makes no difference. (Helpful Hint: If you get more strands in your hands than you can manage, try putting some in your mouth, between your knees and under your arm pits.)

However, if at any time you lose a strand of baling twine and it falls off the hay wagon, you must be prepared to lose life and limb to save that twine. Even though they already have a pile the size of Mount Everest in the barn yard, jumping in front of charging bulls to rescue a strand, walking into the middle of a herd of mad cows or even getting into a tug-o-war with a cow that has half swallowed a strand is nothing compared to the ire demonstrated by a rancher when you lose one of his precious stands of twine. (Helpful Hint: Don't lose any twine.)

Once you have finished feeding the cattle, the group of strands are then folded in half, with ends perfectly even (no compromises allowed here) and tied. (Helpful hint: When there are no ranchers looking, you can slip into the barn and stretch your twines out on the floor to make sure both ends are even. To be even more precise you can tack a yardstick down on the floor to measure each strand. Most ranchers won't even notice that you put it there because men are always measuring stuff anyway.)

Tying the twine involves collecting the folded ends into one hand, giving them one twist, (again I'm not sure why, but you don't want to suffer the consequences of not performing this step) wrapping the loop around the strands forming a hole and pulling the loop through the hole and drawing both ends snug.

They are then gingerly carried by the looped end to the heap and flung on top of the decaying pile of twine to be utilized another day.

As you can see there's really nothing to it, but if it seems like it's taking you a long time to learn this ancient art, don't worry, ranchers seem to enjoy telling people what to do.

Dressed To The Canines

When we inherited a stray puppy last summer we knew she was some kind of Black Lab cross, but we didn't know what she was crossed with. Now at about nine months we are beginning to wonder if she's some kind of miracle mutation because she eats like a horse, is as big as an elephant, leaps like a frog and runs like a cheetah. We thought at one point that she may even have a little skunk in her until we realized it was "on" her.

Needless to say, whatever she is, Puddin' Head has ingratiated herself into most of the family and seems to be a permanent fixture. I say "most of the family" because Skippy the two-foot-long-dog (Dachshund) doesn't seem to care much for her. But that's just because Puddin' tries to play "lion tamer." She puts Skippy's entire head in her mouth and roars. Well... it's more of a sound like a coyote howling backwards, but you get the picture.

I keep telling Skippy to just ignore her, but I guess it's pretty hard to ignore someone who's giving you an unsolicited close-up view of her esophagus.

Oh, and did I mention Puddin' has the breath of a wild boar with gingivitis? Skippy usually sneezes and snorts for a good five minutes after one of the lion taming sessions.

Fortunately, for Skippy, she has built in clothing and doesn't have to put up with Puddin while trying to get dressed every morning. I would almost trade places with her and take on the lioness puppy if it wasn't for the canine halitosis.

My troubles begin the minute I step out of the shower, which opens directly into our bedroom. Puddin' grabs my towel and after a rousting few minutes of tug-o-war, which she always wins because I don't want to rip the towel, she takes off with it. That's when she demonstrates her agile cheetah-like qualities by diving under the bed and ducking behind dressers at lightning speeds with me chasing her. By the time I finally get the towel away from her I've air-dried from running around so much that I don't need it any more.

Trying to put pants on is a major chore because she grabs a pant leg and seals the opening shut like a zip lock baggie and I can't get my foot through. Although this gives me an opportunity to practice my balancing skills, I can only do it for so long before falling on the floor.

While I'm lying on the floor, she stands guard over me. Every time I try to get up she slurps my face with her big wet tongue and the smell of her breath is enough to knock me back down again. My only recourse is to treat her like a bear and play dead until she tires of trying and wanders off.

When it comes time for shoes and socks she comes back full-force. She's made a pretty good game of the socks — I put one on and she patiently waits until I'm in the middle of putting the other one on, and then pulls the first one off. This can go on for ten minutes until I finally manage to get a shoe on one foot. She's gotten smarter though, and when she sees the shoe going on she knows the sock game is about to come to an end so she grabs my other shoe and takes off with it.

Thus begins the new game "Find the Shoe." She follows me around the house smiling and wagging her tail as I search behind chairs, under tables and in closets. She tries to throw me off track by darting her eyes around the room thinking that I will go in the direction she's looking. One time she hid my shoe in the toilet —I no longer own that shoe — and another time she put it in the Kitchen Aid mixer — that shoe almost wound up in a batch of muffins.

She's getting better at hiding my shoes as time goes on and there are some that I haven't been able to find for three months. I suspect that maybe she's buried a few out in the pasture, which I hope will turn up this week while we're harrowing.

I've actually had to go to work with mismatched shoes because after several mornings of not having time to look for lost shoes, I couldn't find two that were the same. And at my age it sounds pretty lame to show up late for work and say, "My dog stole my shoe and I couldn't find it." That's almost as bad as being in high school and using the excuse that my dog ate my assignment, which I'm sure Puddin' Head would do given the chance.

So a lot of times I go limping into work with mismatched shoes, one sock, slobbered on pants and wet hair. The thing that kind of has me worried though is that no one at work seems to notice....

Chicken Poop
For The Soles

A ll ranchers have to have chickens at least once in their lives... in order to appreciate not having them.

My experience with chickens began about ten years ago. It started out with a simple desire to have fresh eggs and turned into a cluckish nightmare.

It took four years of begging to talk my husband, Mike, into letting me have chickens. He had the usual concerns — who was going to take care of them, who was going to take care of them, and then there was the problem of — who was going to take care of them.

Once I convinced him that the chickens would be my responsibility and he wouldn't have to lift a finger, I set him to work building the chicken coop of my dreams.

Wisely deciding to save money, Mike bought an old chicken coop that was in dire need of repair for $50 from our neighbors. He figured we could replace a few old weathered boards here and there and it would be good as new. Five hundred dollars and three weeks later, we had a coop that any rooster and his flock of hens would be proud of.

After I finally got Mike to stop calculating how many eggs it would take to amount to $500, adding in the cost of chicken feed and multiplying it by how many hours he worked, I entered into the world of poultry. I purchased two Barred Rock roosters and 12 young hens and introduced them to their new home — my spotless, freshly painted chicken coop turned into a coop full of chicken poop in about five minutes. No wonder they are called fowl.

Before getting my own chickens, people had told me of the wonderful benefits of chicken fertilizer for gardens. Now I realize the reason they always tried to talk it up was because they were hoping I would take some of the stuff. What do you do with ten tons of chicken poop?

Before long every square inch of property we had was fertilized with the white essence of chickens and it became harder and harder to think of ways to dispose of it, although we got rid of a lot of it on the soles of our shoes. It got to the point that when we were invited to a potluck dinner, I would take a macaroni salad, baked beans, and a pickup bed full of chicken poop as a hostess gift.

All of that seemed irrelevant though when I went to the chicken house one morning and found the first egg. I was so excited I ran to the house and cooked it for breakfast. Mike and I marveled for hours about how much more yellow the yolk looked and how much better it tasted, but mainly, that if there was only one the next day — who was going to get to eat it.

So began the daily routine of scooping poop and skipping off to the chicken coop with a basket to gather eggs. In the process however, I did make one startling discovery — chickens don't want you to take their eggs. Within a week my hands were completely covered with chicken peck marks. When people would ask about my hands, I wanted desperately to say that I had tangled with a cougar or even a wild barn cat to avoid the disappointed looks that came when I said, "chickens did it."

It then became a challenge to avoid those ferocious pecking, pinching beaks. I tried several things: welder's gloves were too bulky and I couldn't pick up the eggs, letting them eat chicken food out of one hand while I tried to snatch the eggs with the other, just proved they were faster than me, and trying to raise them off their nests with a Handyman Jack... Well... let's just say chickens fly at your face when they are really mad.

The only thing that did work was taking my dog into the coop as a diversion — the chickens would fly off of their nests and chase the dog out the door, leaving me free to gather the eggs. After two or three times, just when I thought I had it figured out, the dog started mysteriously disappearing every morning and didn't return until noon.

Then one day after searching catalogs for implements used in chicken warfare and ruling out options like a Hazmat suit and a mechanical robot, I got this horrendous itch right in the middle of my back. I reached for this wooden backscratcher that we had with a hand-shaped claw, and an idea hit me. I ran out to the chicken house to try it out. I found that I could stand two feet away from the chickens, slip the hand end of the scratcher underneath a nesting hen and drag the eggs out from under her into a padded basket. The hens still pecked like crazy, but put dents into the wooden backscratcher instead of me. It worked like a charm.

Gradually the dog started coming around again, we had fresh eggs every morning for breakfast, and after about five years, Mike finally put away his calculator.

But that wasn't the end of the chicken fiasco. One of the roosters unexpectedly died and the remaining rooster, who unaffectionately came to be known as "Rambo the Rooster" took over the hen house. Now that the hen harem was all his, he passionately protected them from any predators or egg thieves such as myself.

For several weeks as he was sizing me up, he strutted around the coop flapping and squawking at me. Then one day, he couldn't take the act of me gathering up his potential offspring any longer, and he snapped. He flew up and attacked my backscratcher, biting, pecking and clawing like a rooster gone bad. We fenced like sword fighters — he with his beak and me with my trusty backscratcher until he broke my scratcher in half. He spat out his half and came at me with an aerial assault. Realizing that I was no match for this savior of poultry, I made a hasty exit.

For days after the battle I avoided the chicken coop for fear of Rambo. I gave myself pep talks to try and work up the nerve to no avail— "it's just a little chicken, it can't hurt you, now go out there and get those eggs." Then one day I realized that if I didn't get the eggs, there would be baby chicks

57

hatching, which meant more chicken poop — that gave me the courage — the fear of more poop.

So I went out to the chicken coop, this time taking a farmwife's weapon – a broom. I originally wanted to take the shotgun but Mike wouldn't let me have it. I put on rubber boots and gloves, rolled up my sleeves, and literally swept the coop clean of chickens including Rambo the Rooster, who was no match for my nylon angled Broommaster. Rambo kept trying to come back in the coop and I kept sweeping him out the door where he landed on his chicken backside until he finally conceded to the power of the broom.

Everyday after that, all I had to do was flash my broom and Rambo would listlessly strut to the corner of the coop and watch me with his beady eyes as I gathered the eggs — with a brand new unbreakable backscratcher.

When Cow Dogs
Go To Town

R anchers are often misunderstood in urbanized communities. For instance, city folks don't understand why we have to have at least two cow dogs in the back of our trucks at all times, even when there are seemingly no cows around. But even in the city we never know when we might encounter a cow…. And encountering a cow without a cow dog is like encountering a pile of spaghetti noodles without a fork.

You never know, we could be driving along and all of the sudden spot a wayward cow going into a Wal-Mart store. Without a rancher and his trusty dogs to round it up and head it out, the cow could browse the kitchen utensil aisle indefinitely.

And since all cows have the ability to *charge*, she could rack up quite a bill. But cows aren't freeloaders and generally would compensate by making a certain type of *deposit* on the floor. In fact, an overly generous cow could leave several scattered throughout the store.

On the plus side, she would leave a farm-like aroma, which would make us ranchers feel much more at home while shopping in the store. For some reason, which continues to baffle ranchers, city folks don't seem to like that eau-de-cow-pooh-pooh perfume.

In fact I have had several people blatantly turn up their noses when I enter a store with the fragrant bovine cologne on my boot. I've since decided that it's not worth the effort any more to go out and find the ripest pile in the field and step in it before going to town, city folks just don't seem to appreciate it like our ranching neighbors.

However, owners could really benefit from the ranching community if they would allow us to bring our cow dogs into their stores. Not only could we round up wayward cows, but as an added bonus two or three good urban cow dogs could round up customers at closing time and herd them through the checkout lines.

Cow dogs could also keep an eye on employees that had a tendency toward laziness. There's nothing like a good nip on the heels to get a person moving.

And if business is particularly slow, two cow dogs could work both sides of the street to herd people walking by into the store. Once in the store the dogs could drive them toward the sale items.

Cow dogs could also save money by allowing a business owner to hire fewer employees.

For instance in a grocery store, instead of announcing, "Clean up on aisle five," when someone drops a jar of ketchup or breaks open a bag of Doritos, a group of cow dogs could be sent to gobble up the mess in about two seconds flat and herd the clumsy customer out the door before they have a chance to break anything else.

In restaurants, cow dogs could save a lot of time by hovering under the tables and eating anything that falls on the floor. They could also keep customers away from their plates, even if they aren't finished eating, when waitresses want to take them.

People could even use cow dogs to solve a problem with the "unsightly view," which is common when hiring help to work on their homes. Every time a plumber or other construction worker stoops or bends over, the dogs could make them stand up until their britches were properly adjusted for the task.

But where a cow dog would really shine is on a used car lot. They already have a gold chain around their necks and they could herd potential buyers into the office and nip at their heels until they sign a contract.

It's Duck Season...

S traying from our usual ranch related activities, my husband, Mike, and I decided to try out our hunting skills last weekend.

We somehow inherited an abandoned puppy several weeks ago, and Mike has a rule, which he tries to enforce to no avail, that every unit of livestock or animal in our possession has to be earning its keep. Therefore we won't mention the four year-old bummer lamb that we couldn't part with, the horse that couldn't be ridden or the barren old cow that he says has a "cute face." But this puppy, among other things, looks like it may have some black lab in it, therefore Mike has announced that she will be a hunting dog and not for just any kind of hunting, but duck hunting. Keep in mind we have never hunted ducks before, but now feel compelled to do so.

So the adventure begins with the usual preparations of cleaning cobwebs out of shotguns that we haven't used in five years and Mike informing me that this puppy, the one he said he didn't want to have anything to do with when we got her, is now his dog. "I will be in charge of all of the training," he said. "Puddin' Head's (that's the dignified name we gave her) too young to let loose so I'll put her on a leash and try and get her used to everything — you can just carry your gun and watch for ducks — I'll be in charge of Puddin'."

After getting that straight, we headed for the river with plans to walk along the banks, scare up some ducks and have them for dinner.

As we sneaked noiselessly along the riverbank, Mike got into character with his imitation of Elmer Fudd. "Be very, very, quiet," he's says. "I'm hunting ducks." Playing along, as Daffy Duck, I said, "It's wabbit season," which began a ten-minute reenactment of Looney Tunes, which we are thankful no one was around to hear.

Just as he was crouching down and going through, the "be very, very quiet" routine, Mike accidentally stepped on the dog's foot and Puddin' Head yelped and whined at ear-breaking decimals for a good five minutes while every duck within a mile bolted from the river.

I raised my shotgun to shoot and by the time I remembered where my safety was, the ducks were gone. Meanwhile, Mike was trying to untangle the leash, which the dog had wrapped around and in between his legs, while wielding a shotgun in the air and cursing the waterfowl.

Undaunted by this little turn of events, Mike said the ducks would land farther up the river and we would just have to walk a few more miles than we had anticipated to find them again. Thus ended the Looney Tunes episode and we became serious about duck hunting.

As it turns out, Mike was correct, and we did encounter the ducks again. This time we spotted them long before they saw us, and Mike instructed me to hold the dog, while he assumed the shooting position.

Having received my orders earlier about who was in charge of the dog, I said, "No can do." Puzzled by this recent turn of events, Mike said, "And why not?" As I began the lengthy reenactment of his previous orders complete with quotes, hand waving and the inherited Schoeningh stagger that males of the family perform to make a point, about 50 ducks flew up from the river again and were headed right for us. We tied the dog to the nearest tree and began blasting away as they flew overhead.

You can imagine our surprise when the gun smoke cleared and we realized we didn't hit a single one. Mike just shrugged his shoulders, grabbed the dog, reloaded his gun and said, "Be very, very quiet. I'm hunting wabbits."

Duck, It's Not What's For Dinner

N ow that my husband, Mike, and I have decided to officially announce our decision to become "duck hunters," other ranchers are slowly coming out of the closet. Most people wouldn't think twice about someone hunting ducks, but for ranchers, it's like being unfaithful to the cattle industry.

Although you will occasionally catch a rancher sneaking a piece of chicken or gnawing on a rack of pork ribs, (ranchers will argue that anything herdable is still livestock) they will go to great lengths to conceal their appetite for hunting wild game, especially duck. Not only because it's not beef, but because duck tastes like an old leather boot that was walked in hard without any odor eaters. We know this not because we have actually shot and hit one, but because we had the unfortunate experience of being the recipients of a gift duck.

One day a couple of years ago, Mike and I were in the hardware/sporting goods store and we witnessed just how far ranchers will go to cover up their duckly intentions.

Our neighbor, Billy Bob McKrackin, a portly fellow and lifelong participant of the bib overall fashion craze, was buying duck decoys when Vern Mudswallow, a local Brand Inspector, spied him. He was just on his way to the checkout counter with a duck stuffed under each arm when Vern caught him.

"Whatcha' got there Billy Bob?" asked Vern.

"Oh this...this here's a plastic duck," says Billy Bob holding out one of them for Vern to see.

"I can see that," says Vern. "But what are you going to do with it?"

Relying on the excuse he had concocted long before he arrived at the store Billy Bob says, "The wife wanted some new lawn ornaments and I thought these little ducks would look nice out by her bird fountain."

"Whew," says Vern. "For a minute there I thought you were fixing to go duck hunting."

"Oh no, I'm a beef man myself," says Billy Bob. "Got that registered herd of Angus you know. We never eat anything but beef. Why my daddy always used to say there's nothing like a good beefsteak to cure what ails you...." About that time the store clerk interrupted the conversation and looked Billy Bob straight in the eye saying, "Are you purchasing these 12-gauge shot shells sir and this duck call?"

Billy Bob stammered for a moment and was about to think up another excuse, but he realized they really weren't his. "No ma'am just need these ducks for my wife's flower bed," he says.

Then looking over at Vern to see if he had given anything away, he noticed perspiration was starting to bead up on Vern's upper lip. All of the sudden Vern didn't look very well. He was just about to ask Vern if he was okay when Vern managed to say in a croaked voice, "I believe those are mine ma'am. But I didn't know that was a duck call. I ... er...aah... thought it was one of those calls you use to attract coyotes." He turned to Billy Bob and nervously said, "Coyotes have been coming in too close to the calves lately and I thought I would pepper them with a little buck shot to scare them off."

Billy Bob nodded in agreement, as he and Vern exchanged a knowing look — both realizing without speaking, that the other knew what they weren't supposed to know and each acting as if they didn't know – that they were both fixing to go duck hunting.

It's hard to determine why they couldn't just both admit they were hunting ducks, at least to each other. To this day we've actually seen them both out hunting, separately of course, but don't dare ask them if they've bagged any ducks.

But fortunately, times are changing and ranchers are getting to the point that they no longer have to restrict all of their activities to the raising and eating of livestock to avoid being scorned by their peers. At some point we will even be able to have hunting dogs like black labs and golden retrievers without insisting that they "do too make good stock dogs."

Mike and I have been hunting now for several weeks and have heard some of the name calling that has been going on from certain members of the ranching community — names like "duck eaters unlimited," "mallard munchers," or "fowl weather ranchers," have crossed our ears more than once.

To date though, we haven't been able to bring down a single bird, no doubt due to faulty shells and or guns, bad weather, unrealistic duck decoys, a hunting dog that barks every time it sees a duck, and all the usual maladies facing duck hunters — I'm sure it has nothing to do with our abilities as hunters

But if we could hit just one of the blasted flat-billed, quacking $#@!!s, we have plans to give it to Billy Bob. Not only to see his reaction, but because we sure wouldn't want to have to eat it ourselves.

Entrepreneurs At Large

There comes a time in almost every ranch wife's life when she makes this crucial statement, "I want money of my own to spend on whatever I want instead of on salt blocks and calf scour medicine." That usually comes about the time when you tell your husband you are going to buy a new dress and he says, "Why bother? The cows don't care how you look anyway."

My good friend and ranching neighbor, Nina, and I reached that critical moment about six years ago, and even though we both have very kind, loving and considerate husbands, who will usually give us what we want if we cry, throw a fit and threaten not to help with spring branding or harrowing, we decided two things: we wanted money that we didn't have to throw into the "general ranching fund" and we didn't want to have to leave home to get it.

As we started to compile our collective cash-producing ideas we speculated that not only could we make spending money for ourselves, but heck, our ideas were so good we could just imagine the look of disbelief on our husband's faces when we began presenting them with things like new tractors and what every rancher wants — more cows.

So our adventures began when one of us — not to name names, but the one that is not me — heard about a local clothes designer who needed people to sew dresses. It sounded like the perfect setup, the material and patterns were provided, so there would be no out-of-ranch expenses — just our time. And Nina and I had so much experience sewing ripped jeans that we figured we qualified as seamstresses.

We set up shop in Nina's living room and spread our first assignment out on the carpet. The fabric was so beautiful, shiny and satiny that we felt like we had already moved up in financial status just by handling it.

Once the pattern was cut out we divided up the pieces, sat down at our machines and began to happily calculate the profits as we sewed. We decided to shoot for five dresses a day, sewing five days a week. It seemed so simple we wondered why other ranch wives hadn't hit upon this idea yet.

Our first indication of why everyone in the valley wasn't doing this came when we realized about five minutes into the project that expensive, shiny, satiny fabric is so slick it slides right off the sewing machine.

After sewing my first few seams I proudly laid my garment out for Nina to inspect. The seams were nice and straight and the appropriate width so it was easy to see that my high school Home-Ec classes had paid off. But on further inspection Nina said, "There's just one problem... How are you going to put it on?"

I said, "Well, don't forget, we still have to put the zipper in."

"Yes," she said. "But where are the neck and arm holes?"

Being optimistic, I said, "Maybe it's a wrap around."

It was at this point that I became familiar with a little tool known as the seam ripper. By the end of the day we were both contemplating changing our business from seamstresses to professional seam rippers.

But we persevered and after working six to eight hours a day for five days we had completed one whole dress. We added up our hours and calculated our profits for the week and found that we were actually paying the dress designer who had hired us $6 an hour for the privilege of sewing for her. At that rate we figured we would have to starting selling our husband's tractors to pay her off rather than buying them new ones.

So we decided to try other ideas. There were the homemade scented bath salts in decorative jars, which turned out beautifully. But when we decided it might be a good idea to try out the product ourselves, we bent several spoons trying to get the bath salts out of the jars — they had set up hard as a rock overnight.

Then came the soap. We had read an article in a magazine about a woman who was making a living off selling decorative scented soap. Since we had already spent our life's savings on scents for the bath salts we thought this would be a prudent move, until we looked at the soap making process and discovered that you had to use lye. Which one of us was going to be in charge of handling the toxic chemical? Since I couldn't convince Nina that she should be the one, we realized that neither one of us could probably afford to become badly burned.

So we looked at the process and decided that if soap began as a liquid and then hardened, maybe the process would work in reverse. We purchased about 20 bars of a well-known brand of soap, cut them up into pieces and put them in pans on the stove to melt. It would have been a great idea if Soft Soap hadn't already been invented — we poured it into candle forms and it never did return to its hardened state even after we put it in the freezer. It did however ruin a few good pans and make everything in the freezer taste like soap for weeks.

There were several other things we tried, like candles — we already had the forms from the soap and the scented oils from the salts — but we couldn't get enough money out of them to make it lucrative. We also tried something we thought every woman would want — decoratively painted wooden needle cases — and soon discovered that apparently every woman really doesn't want them. I think Nina still has about 200 of them in her attic.

We even tried a farming and ranching newsletter, but the post office box that we rented for a year to send them out of (we didn't want thousands of subscriptions piling up in our own mailing boxes) expired before we got our first newsletter finished.

There was also the hand-sewn fabric greeting cards — took two weeks to make one $3 card. The rubber stamp greeting cards were also a flop because everyone could buy the stamps and make them cheaper than we could sell them for.

We thought we had really come up with a winner though when we hit up on the idea of homemade pre-packaged calf scour medicine. A lot of ranchers make their own remedies so we figured out a way to mix all of the ingredients in dry form and all they would have to do was add water — we thought we were brilliant! Turned out the USDA didn't think so...There was something mentioned about fines, licensing and pre-approved animal-safe products...who would have thought?

We finally exhausted all our ideas and ended up getting regular jobs in town to earn our extra income and pay for all the stuff we bought while trying to make money. But we're still looking for that million-dollar idea and having a lot of fun in the process.

I saw Nina in the grocery store the other day and she came up to me and clandestinely whispered, "Measuring spoons — think about it." We gave each other a knowing nod as we began to contemplate those new tractors again — this could be the one that makes us rich!

Name Games And Phone Pains

R anchers have at least one thing in common with the rest of the world — they don't like to get sales calls during dinnertime. Fortunately my husband, Mike, and I have come up with a plan that seems to work pretty well.

Most telemarketers can't pronounce our German name, Schoeningh, so when someone calls and asks for Mr. or Mrs. Shoendinger or Shoeflinger, we politely say, "I'm sorry there's nobody here by that name." It's honest and it works...well, most of the time.

One night we were just sitting down to dinner and the phone rang. Mike answers and the caller asks for Mike Shutnigh. Mike gives our now standard reply, and the caller politely says, "Oh I'm sorry, someone gave me this number and said you had a horse for sale."

Mike says, "Uhhhh... hold on a minute... that's me. I'm Mike Shutnigh, I mean Schoeningh. I do have a horse for sale and he's really nice."

He tried to explain to the caller that he thought she was a telemarketer and that she should come and see the horse for herself, but for some reason there seemed to be a credibility issue and she refused the invitation.

Another thing ranchers, and I'm sure others don't like, is to play the phone options game — it cuts into our playing with cows time.

I tried to find out some information about my cell phone bill the other day by calling the company. After listening to a long list of options like push 1 if you want to purchase phone accessories, push 2 if you want to pay a bill or push 3 if you want to open a new account, I finally chose to push button number 5, which was for "other options," because none of the others appeared to fit my particular circumstance. After a couple of clicks and hums, a recorded voice came on the line and said, "There are no other options available." Like I really needed to know that!

So I went back to the main menu, which was option number 6 and pushed button number 4 to speak to a customer service representative. A recording came on, which said, "There are no representatives available at this time," and it immediately transferred me back to the main menu to select another option.

Persistence paid off though and ten minutes and 42 button pushes later, I did connect to a live person, or at least I think she was alive.

She asked me for the following information: my name, spouse's name, mother's maiden name, cell phone number, regular phone number, social security number, date of birth, and finally for my address. Everything was going well as I correctly answered the information — until I recited my address.

"That's not the address I have for you ma'am," she said.

"Well, what address do you have for me?" I replied."

"I'm not allowed to give out that information, ma'am," she said.

"You've been sending the bill to my address every month for over a year and I've been receiving it," I said. "Is the address I just gave you anywhere close to what you have?"

"I'm not allowed to give out that information ma'am," she again replied.

"Well okay forget the address then," I said. "I just need to know why you didn't credit me for my free minutes on my cell phone this month."

"I'm sorry ma'am," she said. "I'm not allowed to give you that information."

"Why not?" I asked.

"Because you don't know your correct address ma'am," she said.

Sensing my growing irritation she added, "Would you like to speak to my supervisor?"

Ten minutes later another voice comes on the phone, "This is Senior Supervisor Ms. Crankendorf, how may I help you?"

So I explained to Crankendorf that I didn't get credit for my free minutes this month and wanted to know why.

She said, "I'm sure I can help you, let me look up your account." A few minutes later she exclaims, "Oh, I see the problem, but for security reasons, what is your address?"

Thinking, I reached the right person and that I'm finally getting somewhere, I give her my address to which she promptly replies, "I'm sorry ma'am that is not the address that I have for you. I can't give out your account information.

"Okay," I said. "Is there anything at all that you can tell me?"

She said, "I can tell you that you have a bill of $62.47 due. How would you like to pay for that? We accept most major credit cards."

I said, "I'm sorry ma'am but I'm not allowed to give out that information!"

Zucchini Snacks And Belly Tracks

There are some dogs that you just can't help but wish they would have been with you forever. Sergeant Eric Von Schultz was one dog that we will never forget. He succumbed to old age a few years ago, but we often reminisce about the loveable little Dachshund that was as big around as he was long.

The Sergeant became a part of our family when he was about ten years old and by that time his stomach was already so big that it drug the ground making belly tracks wherever he went. He walked like a severely pregnant female with his rear toes turned in and visitors, unable to determine his gender at first glance, would always ask when he was due to whelp.

Although that belly matched nicely with his sweet, good-natured disposition, it was that belly and the insatiable appetite that accompanied it that was always getting him into trouble.

We tried putting him on diets throughout the years, but he would always manage to find alternative sources of food.

He grew up in the city but soon discovered that on a ranch there are always things to eat — never mind if it was nutritional or digestible or even remotely part of the food groups — he would eat it as long as it was filling. Hay, old leather harnesses and empty oat sacks became some of his favorite staples.

At one point during our attempt at rationing out the recommended portions of dog food specifically made for inactive overweight dogs, we had company visiting and were standing out in the yard. Schultz came up from the creek that runs through our property with an eight-inch trout flapping in his jowls.

As the visitors stared in disbelief, my husband, Mike, casually said, "Been fishing, Sergeant?" Schultz just stopped long enough to wag his tail before waddling off with his catch of the day.

As his diet progressed, he took to chasing the chickens around the yard, lumbering after them in his comical lope that was required to take his belly along with him wherever he went. He was always hoping to grab a nugget or a drumstick, but usually ended up with a peck on the head, which sent him scurrying back to the house yipping and yapping all the way about his unfortunate turn of events.

One time while Mike and I were weeding the garden we discovered that a gopher or a ground squirrel had been chewing on the vegetables. The problem soon escalated to the point that every morning we would find that a varmint had been devouring some of our best greens the night before. Not knowing exactly what we were dealing with, we devised a plan to sneak out to the garden late at night with flashlights and see if we could catch the little animal in action.

We crept silently to the edge of the garden and could hear the sound of something munching and smacking away. We zeroed in on the noise and surrounded the animal, both flipping on our lights at the same to time to expose the midnight marauder — and there was Schultz gnawing on a big zucchini — at least he was sticking to his diet.

The most trouble his belly ever got him into though was when he decided that a gopher that had been tearing up the back yard would make a tasty morsel. He spent the better part of a morning digging after it until the gopher finally popped up from a hole and the chase was on.

We could hear him from the house where we were having lunch as he went into his hound dog baying routine in hot pursuit of dinner. After awhile his baying turned into a muffled mournful howl and we went out to see what was going on.

We could hear him, but we couldn't see him anywhere. He sounded like he was really far away, yet we knew he was somewhere in the back yard. As we continued our search, Mike said he could feel a vibration under his feet whenever Schultz would howl.

We finally found him. Apparently during the chase, the gopher had darted through a plastic irrigation pipe that was buried in our back yard to transport ditch water to the nearby orchard. Schultz, not being one to give up easy when he sensed there was the possibility of food, dove in after the animal. There wasn't any water in the pipe at the time, but Schultz misjudged the size of his belly as usual and became wedged right in the middle of the eight-foot long pipe and couldn't get out.

We could lie on the ground and reach in from both ends and almost touch him, but couldn't get a firm enough grip on anything to try and pull or push him out. We tried putting a long leather strap into the pipe, which we knew Schultz even in his predicament would chomp down on not wanting to waste an opportunity to try and eat something and tried pulling him out by his teeth.

We gave up after a few unsuccessful attempts and finally bit the bullet and dug out the entire pipe. Fortunately he was located at a seam and we were able to break the pipe open, and like a yolk falling out of a cracked egg, he hit the ground with a thud.

Less than a second later, undaunted by the whole experience, he was up and running trying to find the gopher scent again.

We replaced the pipe with a larger one that would accommodate his belly, which was a good thing, because he spent a lot of time over the ensuing years chasing varmints through it.

We also eventually gave up on the diet program, because we had no idea of what he might try to eat next and let him live out his last years fat and happy at his favorite pastime, chasing Nilla-Vanilla Wafers across the living room floor.

Guide To Sleep
Deprived Ranchers

S pring-calving ranchers are at the height of their production season right now with the fruits of their labor dropping all over the ground. They are also at the height of their sleep deprivation.

Studies have shown that sleep-deprived ranchers are more likely to walk into walls, kiss the dog and pat their spouse on the head, and use hair spray for underarm deodorant than those ranchers who get enough sleep.

During a night of calving season, ranchers will normally get approximately two hours of sleep. They are actually in bed for five hours, but spend three of those hours worrying about the cows even though they just checked them. The only things that will cause a rancher to worry more are water, taxes, and whether or not the teenager shut the gate to the bullpen.

The calving days are usually uneventful and cows have been known to actually stand cross-legged all day to avoid shooting out a calf before nightfall. Cows are also good at predicting the weather and if a cow suspects she is about to go into labor and there is a forecast of snow, she will hold off giving birth until there are a good two or three inches of snow on the ground, and then will only consider letting go of her offspring if the wind has picked up to around 40 mph.

You may wonder why a cow would want to have a calf in these less than perfect conditions. The truth is they feel an obligation to the rancher who has been feeding them day in and day out, to include him, if not in the actual birthing process, then in the survival of the calf — why should they have all the fun?

So as you can see this is a difficult time for some, and there are several things to consider when encountering a sleep-deprived rancher.

First, never engage a sleep-deprived rancher in a lengthy conversation, as he will nod off in mid-sentence. Keep your questions in a format that will allow them to answer with a yes, no, or a simple grunt.

Never ask a sleep-deprived rancher how his calving is going. Doing so could raise his blood pressure to dangerous levels. If you should forget this rule, back away slowly. Do not try to change the subject. Your best defense is to leave. He probably won't even notice you have gone for quite some time as he continues his cow tirade.

If you encounter a rancher that has fallen asleep, do not attempt to wake him. I repeat, do not attempt to wake him — this is for your own safety. Waking a sleep-deprived rancher, who has finally managed to catch a few zzzz's is similar to waking a hibernating bear two months early. This rule also applies to veterinarians who are found scattered along the roads asleep in their vehicles. It may be tempting to wake them, but remember this is their only refuge from the sleep-deprived ranchers.

If you have a sleep-deprived rancher living in your home, rearrange all of the furniture during this time so it is flat against the walls. This will avoid having them wake you up by their yelling and cursing in the middle of the night after they have stubbed their toe or banged their hip on obviously what should have "never been in their way in the first place," on their way out to check the cows.

And finally, be patient with sleep-deprived ranchers, calving season only lasts a couple of months and then they will be back to normal — until haying season starts...

Wiener Dogs Rule

There are certain things that every rancher needs to be successful and we have found our wiener dogs (Dachshunds) to be an essential tool in our cow/calf operation. The dogs haven't received a great deal of attention in the ranching community; in fact, very few ranchers even realize the advantages of adding one or more of the long bodied canines to their outfit.

Traditional ranch dogs like the Border Collie and Blue Heeler definitely have their place on most ranches, but there are certain things wiener dogs can do that the larger cow dogs can't. For instance, when you are trying to bring cows into the corrals, wiener dogs will actually stand in front of an open gate, yipping and yapping to block cows from going through it. The ear shattering sound irritates the cows so much that they will turn and run the other direction — usually back to the pasture they came from.

Since you initially wanted the cows to go through that gate, here's where it takes a little more thought to figure out how the wiener dogs actually helped. It's already mid-morning and when you calculate how long it will take to gather the cows again, and then vaccinate them, you decide to wait and do it another day — thus the dogs have saved you from having to work the rest of the day!

There are several other reasons that ranchers may want to include wiener dogs in their ranching program. Here are just a few:

The dogs will provide hours of entertainment for your calves. To calves the dogs look like some kind of strange rodent and will romp and play as they chase the dogs around the pastures. One word of caution — if you are trying to put weight on your calves you may need to monitor this activity closely.

Wiener dogs are also invaluable help during haying time. If you take them in the swather with you, they will actually shove you off of the seat and take over the steering, giving you a much needed rest. They can't reach the pedals, but since you are on the floor anyway, you can listen to the dog's signals and pretty well tell when to apply pressure on the appropriate peddle. It takes some practice to discern the yipping, which generally means "give it more gas" from the yapping, which indicates you are about ready to run through a fence. If the yapping is really loud and the dog joins you on the floor licking your face, then you have probably already run through the fence.

Keeping the hay fields free of mice and other small rodents is another important task performed by the dogs. They are great hunters and if you don't see them catch and eat their prey, don't worry — they will come into the house and produce it again for you on the living room carpet.

Wiener dogs are also very adept swimmers (thus the term "water wienies") and routinely dive into irrigation ditches, mud puddles, and your water glass if you set it down. They have a built-in divining rod and are able to search out water that is invisible to the human eye.

This is especially good on a hot day because any amount of water the dog finds he will save on his coat and share it with you by jumping on your lap and shaking all over. The dogs can hold approximately 30 times their body weight in water on their fur. I mention this characteristic because in a drought year like this one, a rancher could send several wiener dogs to the neighbor's irrigation ditches to get water and have them bring it back to shake on his hay fields — the extra water could be enough to produce a third cutting of hay.

84

Around the barnyard, wiener dogs will gather eggs from the hen house. Not only does it help a great deal to have the dogs take over this chore, it can be used as your principal form of aerobic exercise — you can work up a pretty good sweat in the time it takes to catch one of the dogs running around the yard with an egg in its mouth.

As you can see the wiener dog would be a valuable asset to any ranching operation and there are a multitude of reasons to have one. But it's unwise to own a wiener dog just because "all the other ranchers have one." It takes a big commitment and it's also wise to consider the chain of command, especially if you have more than one wiener dog.

Let's say for instance that you have three: there will be the "top dog," the "number one dog," the "boss dog" and then you. Age makes no difference: even the puppies have higher status than you. If you want to remain the master of your domain, then you are not a good candidate to have a wiener dog, because everyone who does get one finds out quickly that wiener dogs rule.

You Know You're A Rancher When...

T hanks to Jeff Foxworthy we all know how to tell if we're a redneck. But for those of you who wake up every morning, wondering how to tell if you're a rancher — which by the way is completely different from being a redneck — here are a set of guidelines.

You know you're a rancher when:

• You wear your Carhartt overalls to go skiing.

• You replace Band-Aids in your first aid kit with baling twine.

• You don't have to go to Spain to see a bull fight.

• Your barn looks nicer than your house.

• Your bathroom has become an intensive care facility for calves or lambs.

• You pay $300 for a new stock dog and he always stands in the gate you are trying to push the cattle through.

• You think nothing of getting dressed up for dinner and taking the flatbed truck, which is always loaded with hay and covered in cow poop.

• You realize cow poop has become a familiar fragrance and not all that unpleasant. You justify the yellow stains on your Levi's by saying it just gives them that worn look — the look people are paying big bucks for and you get it for free.

• You've come to view hay itch as a minor side effect to the sport of feeding livestock and something that all major athletes get in some form or another.

• You feel sorry for people who have to sit in nice warm offices sipping hot coffee while you're out in the snow when it's 10 degrees below zero and get to breathe in all of that fresh frosty air.

• Going to town for supplies and ditch meetings have become your "social activities."

• You start talking to the cow's stomachs to try and influence the unborn calves to come out during the day instead of at 2 a.m. and are considering writing a book on cow psychology.

• You sell your calves and two days later the price goes up 40 cents a pound.

• Your shovel has become your constant companion and you've named your four-wheeler "Big Red."

• You are down to three horses, one is 29 years old, one is crippled and the 8-year-old that you purchased as a yearling, you haven't had time to break yet.

• Your idea of golf is flipping cow pies out of the yard with a stick.

• Your pile of baling twine is the tallest structure on your property and the neighbors are complaining that it's blocking their view.

• Your personal vehicles were all made before 1982 and the air conditioning consists of rolling down the windows and going 70 mph, but your brand new tractor has "climate control."

• You watch Thursday night Smack Down wrestling to learn new ways to throw a calf.

• You refer to your home office as a command post during irrigation season and when you go out to irrigate the pastures you are on a water recon mission. You won't allow other ranchers into your office during this time as you have secret charts and maps on your walls of your watering strategies and you hold family briefings on what to tell the neighbors if they should ask about water.

• You find yourself practicing your Star Wars light saber skills with a hotshot in the barnyard.

• Your idea of getting dressed up to go to town in the summer months is to turn down the tops of your hip-high irrigation boots.

• You can't ever find your wallet or your car keys, but you know exactly where your shovel is at all times.

• You call all of your cows by name, most of which are not suitable to repeat in public.

• You can recite all of your neighbors' water rights within a 50-mile radius, but can't remember your spouse's birthday or your own.

• You take your family on an outing and you yell to your spouse to "round up the kids and head them out."

• For your wedding anniversary you buy your spouse a new section of sprinkler line every year.

• You have at least one stock dog riding in the back of your pickup at all times, whether it can actually work cattle is not a priority as long as it looks good in your truck.

• You have considered calling the Olympic committee to complain that they don't include the 200 Meter Calf Chase, the Bull Dodge N' Dart or the Fence Hurdles in their Summer Games.

• You dutifully go to church three times a year, Easter, Christmas and at the beginning of irrigation season to pray for rain.

• You know you're a rancher when duct tape and baling twine have become the only items in your toolbox.

• And finally, you know you are a rancher if at the end of the year, when you add up all of your expenses and subtract them from your profits. If you end up with nothing, you can be sure you're a rancher.

Branding, The Musical Version

E very rancher looks forward to calving season, mainly so they can get it over with for the year, and every rancher looks forward to branding time, basically for the same reason.

We recently completed our branding and we're finding that as we get older, help is harder to find. I've ascertained that either it's because we're getting crankier and harder to work with...or we've gone through all of our family and friends over the years and we can no longer convince them that it's "fun." That only seems to work once, and the following year they usually have something more important scheduled to do at that time like replacing their septic tank.

So this year my husband and I worked the cows and branded the calves with the help of our teenage son who so generously offered his assistance (we bribed him by telling him he could drive the four-wheeler and go as fast as he wanted) and my mother who always helps because that's what mothers do.

As I was trying to find a way to describe the day's events, I decided it might best be related in a song and since I'm not a musician or a songwriter, and you can thank your lucky stars that you don't have to hear me sing it either, I worked up this little ditty to the tune of "Git Along Little Doggies."

Git Along Little Doggies And Keep Gittin'

As I was branding one morning cuz I had to,
I spied a white calf amovin' along.
His head was throwed back and his eyes were aglarin',
And as I approached, He was kickin' me strong.

Chorus
Whoop-ee ti-yi-yo, git along little doggies,
It's my misfortune and none of your own.
Whoop-ee ti-yi-yo, git along little doggies,
I know that Safeway will be your new home.

It's early in spring that we round up the doggies,
We call all the relatives that offered to help out.
When those two show we round up our four-wheelers,
And we chase them doggies and cows all about.
(Repeat Chorus)

Once we get the little doggies up into the corrals,
We start poking and prodding and moving them in line.
We mark them and brand them and get stepped on and
leaked on,
And some of them doggies leave a little poop behind.
(Repeat Chorus)

It's whooping and cursing and pushin' the doggies,
And oh how we wish they would go on their own!
It's whooping and punching, and yelling at each other,
But we know that we will soon all get to go home.
(Repeat Chorus)

As the day wears on we try not to use our smellers,
Cuz the doggies are cute, but they stink like a sewer.
And pretty soon we begin to take on that same awful
odor,
By then we were wishing that them doggies were fewer.

(Repeat Chorus)

The cows were nearby just waiting their turn,
We herded them up to be worked in the chute,
They're a little heavier and a lot madder it seems,
We found that out when they stomped on our boot.
(Repeat Chorus)

The days filled with branding are both long and quite
hard,
So we like to complain to almost anyone who can hear.
But the nice thing about it that saves us poor ranchers,
Is that branding fortunately only comes once in a year.
(Repeat Chorus)

Some ranch wives, they go help brand just for pleasure,
But that's where they get it most awfully wrong.
They haven't a notion the trouble doggies give them,
When they begin to find out they start singing this song.

Whoop-ee ti-yi-yo, go brand your own doggies,
It's been my misfortune to come help you along.
Whoop-ee ti-yi-yo, git out of my way,
I'm going to take a bath plumb full of Calgon.

Cold Calves And Toilet Paper Blues

Spring calving is almost over, but it was an eventful one with the two weeks of cold wet weather that we had. Newborn calves can generally stand the cold, but when they are hatched out already wet into the middle of a rainstorm or plopped onto a wet snow bank, they can't get dry and lose their body temperature in no time at all. But fortunately most ranchers are equipped with the IBCU (Intensive Bathroom Calf Unit).

Our IBCU really came in handy this year. Early one morning as I was going through my usual wake-up routine of staring off into space for several minutes while waiting for my brain to become activated, my husband, Mike, came running into the house with a sopping wet calf in his arms. It had been raining most of the night and the poor critter, which had been born about two hours before, was suffering from hypothermia.

I determined this by checking the calf's vital signs — first I gently squeezed his tail and when water leaked out onto the floor, I decided he was too wet for his own good.

Then I checked with the ECT (Emergency Calf Technician, Mike) who brought him in. He reported that this was "one cold calf," which I confirmed by checking his ears (Mike's were cold too) and I said, "Get the calf to IBCU stat!"

As soon as I began prepping the calf for de-hypothermiazation, the ECT came running into IBCU with another calf that appeared to be suffering from the same malady and informed me that he was going out in the field to check for more. Sensing that this situation could easily turn into an epidemic, I relied on the intermom system to call for help — I yelled from the bottom of the stairs to my teenage son, Jake, who has been working with me as a RCA (Reserve Calf Assistant) for several years, "Get out of bed, we have a calf crisis on our hands!"

By the time Jake had stumbled down the stairs in his half-awake mode and we had rushed back to IBCU, Mike had brought in another calf and had taken off to look for more. So Jake and I began working on the three wet ones.

I took an internal temperature reading on the calves, which is more accurate than feeling their ears, by poking my index finger in their mouths to see how cold they were. This scientific test indicated that their status had moved up from cold to "really" cold.

We turned up the furnace and put a portable heater in IBCU on high and shut the door creating an incubator environment. Then we began the tedious task of drying them off with towels while simultaneously rubbing them to get their circulation going. A wet calf can sop up more water than a sponge and takes twice as long to dry.

The calves were starting to recover, but the one Jake was working on seemed to be in critical condition and wasn't responding to routine treatment so we had to get out the heavy duty equipment — the good guest towels and the hair dryer.

Like a surgical nurse I deftly slapped the supplies into Jake's hand as he alternately used the blow dryer and guest towels making his way around the entire calf. When he finished, he placed a heating pad across the calf's ribs and wrapped him up in blankets.

The other two calves didn't need quite as intensive treatment, but at one point we had two hair dryers, a heating pad and the portable heater going all at the same time, which blew a fuse.

We had to argue about which one of us got to get out of the sweltering hot box that we had created in IBCU and go down to the basement where it was cool to reset the breaker switch on the fuse box. In the end he won, because he's faster than me, bigger than me and was nearest the door.

I always look forward to calving season, not only because it's so precious to see the birth of a new creature, but also because I generally lose about five pounds during these IBCU saunas.

Once we had the calves completely dry and warmed up, they still didn't seem to have much energy and just lay limply on the floor. We decided to go have breakfast and check on them in a little while, hoping that they would still be alive.

Right in the middle of the scrambled eggs we heard an awful commotion of bellowing, thrashing and crashing. We jumped up in mid-bite and ran to IBCU and flung open the door to find the three calves standing up with toilet paper strung all over the room looking at us sheepishly from under blankets, which were still partially hanging from them. One had even managed to get himself wedged behind the toilet and couldn't get out. It was an awful mess, but we were so happy to see that they had recovered, all we could do was laugh.

The laughter didn't last long though when we realized the amount of work ahead of us — unfortunately the calves were not potty trained, even though they were in the right room for this, and the wet toilet paper that they had some how managed to string all over the room, was plastered on the floor and walls and had dried on them from the heat in the room.

We called the ECT to come and take them out to the barn and Jake and I began scrubbing the walls with bleach and repairing the torn wallpaper caused by flailing calf hooves. And as for the good guest towels — don't worry — they're now shop rags.

Rancher's Ailments

R anchers suffer common ailments just like the rest of the general population, but there are some that are indigenous to the lifestyle they lead that most city folks don't get exposed to.

Here are just a few of our most common complaints and their causes:

Four-wheeler Thumb — this is characterized by an aching and loss of mobility in the thumb from pressing the gas lever for extended periods of time and is most likely to appear after hours of trying to round up cattle, and typically only happens when you are on the verge of getting the job done. Just when you are about to drive the last of the herd through the gate, the thumb will cramp up, causing you to let go of the gas and lose your momentum while the cows nonchalantly turn and walk in the opposite direction of the gate. If left untreated, Four-wheeler Thumb will rapidly progress to Damn Cowitis where the mouth forms obscene words, which are released at high decibels and aimed directly at cows.

Ditch Water Hands – this is characterized by sore, cracked skin on the hands caused from playing in the water and building dams all day. This is an adult rancher's ailment because children usually grow tired of playing in the water, giving up long before their hands are affected. Ranchers typically don't know when to give up and often continue playing well into the night. Although Ditch Water Hands is not contagious, oddly enough the wife usually develops Throw The Dinner Out The Dooritis as a result of the cause of this ailment.

Swather Snout – this is characterized by intense itching of the nose and prolonged sneezing caused from removing hay that is plugging up the swather header. As the hay is pulled out of the header, it releases a large cloud of grass pollen that is sucked up the unsuspecting rancher's nose. The pollen that doesn't get sucked up the nose lands on the face and hands and is consequently smeared into the eyes as the rancher feverishly rubs his nose. As in the case with Four-wheeler Thumb, this too often progresses to Damn Cowitis and can lead to another well-known ranching malady, Let Them Starveitis.

Baler Whiplash – this is characterized by stiffness and tenderness in the neck and upper back caused by the constant jerking motion of the baler as it works to spit out completed bales of hay. Ranchers will usually spread this contagious ailment by talking the wife into baling halfway through the field. Once the baling is done for the day, the husband will seek relief by asking the wife, who now also has baler whiplash, for a back rub. When she refuses because of her own debilitating symptoms, the tension causes increased back and neck pain for both and often leads to Damn Wifeitis and Insensitive Husbanditis.

Pre and Post Branding Syndrome (PBS) – this is characterized by intense crankiness and mood swings at calf branding time and both the rancher and wife are affected. It is caused by the inability of the wife to read her husband's mind and know exactly where she is supposed to be and what she is supposed to be doing at all times. Some of the symptoms include unprovoked yelling at the wife like, "Why the !@$&! did you let that son of a $@#$! heifer in the pen with the $#@#!$ bulls? Now we have to start sorting them $$!!##&s all over again!" The wife in turn contracts Stomp Back To The Houseitis and the husband eventually winds up with a heaping case of Guiltitis.

Although the medical field has tried unsuccessfully to find cures for these ailments, most ranchers and their wives suffer along and find momentary relief in Whineitis, complaining to anyone who will listen.

That Does Not Compute

W hen it comes to high tech machinery, ranchers are some of the first to try it out if it will help them save time and money in the fields. But, when it comes to computers, they are some of the last ones to succumb to this modern day technology.

Our neighbor, Billy Bob McKrackin, owns a $200,000 tractor that uses a global positioning satellite to program it to make perfectly straight rows. It has a heated seat for the winter with adjustable lumbar support, an air-conditioned cab in the summer, digital readouts on the dash, voice activated commands and a built in flat screen television so he won't miss Oprah. But do you think he would let his wife, Belva, have a computer that would cut her ranch bookkeeping duties in half, better organize their records and save money preparing taxes?

Belva recently told me of her husband's reluctance to entertain the notion of buying a computer, or as she puts it, "his stubborn, mule-headed, nincompoop" attitude toward them.

So I decided to talk to Billy Bob and see just exactly what he does know about computers and why he wouldn't want to own one. One of the things he immediately pointed out was that when he had an opportunity to look at one, he couldn't see much in that "little box" because of the bright glare.

I said, "You know you can get them with 20 inch non-flicker screens now."

He said, "Shoot, a 20 inch screen won't keep the flickers (woodpeckers) off the porch, much less out of your house and away from your computer."

Undaunted by his lack of computer savvy, I pressed on, determined to make him understand what a computer could do for him and Belva. I continued to tell him about several other features on a computer and these are the responses I received:

Backup – "I don't need to know how to back up, I was backing up tractors to the hay pile before you were born."

Cache – "That's what I've been trying to tell you, if I hang on to my cache I can buy a new hay rake instead of a darn computer."

Chips – "Well if chips are worth that much money, I have a whole pasture full of cow chips, and they're a darn sight bigger than those. Just tell me where to send them."

Hardcopy – "Yes it is hard to copy what you're saying, I wish you would speak in plain English."

Keyboard – "I already have a keyboard in the kitchen, that's where I have the keys to my tractor hanging."

Serial Port – "I prefer hard liquor myself."

Windows – "Well just how many windows does a feller need? We've got two or three in every room of the house."

Modem – "Our youngest son already takes care of the front and backyard lawns, so I never have to modem anyway."

Mouse Pad— "Hell, the mice don't need a pad, they're already living in my grain bin."

Disk – "I already have a disk, does a fine job of turning up the fields too."

Internet – "The outside net around the strawberries seems to do a good job of keeping out the varmints, I've never seen any reason to put up an inner-net."

Ram – "No, I've never needed a ram, cuz you see I don't have any ewes, just cows. You wouldn't happen to know where I could get a good bull would you?"

Byte – "I already have a dog that bytes and I've been trying to cure him of so I sure don't need any more. He's got Belva's ankles torn up something awful."

Search Engine — " I've never had any problem finding my engines, I always know right where they're at."

Desktop — "That's what I keep telling Belva. If we put a computer on the desk, we will never be able to find the top of it again."

Server — "Belva's the only server I need and she does a mighty fine job of it too."

Megahertz — Yeah my head's starting to hurt too with all of this computer talk. Would you like to see my new tractor, it's about time for Oprah to start."

Basics Of Cow-Herding Language

A lthough ranchers normally blend in well with the rest of the general population, there are times when they stand out because they speak a different language that is not known to anyone but cows. Because of the complexity of the language, it is only used for special occasions such as moving cattle, forcing them down a chute or into a trailer, and you will rarely hear it used outside of these situations.

But, like the magician who is ostracized by other masters of magic for giving away the trade secrets, I too face an uncertain future in the ranching industry by divulging the translation of this unwritten ranchers lingo. For that reason, to protect my identity I will be using my pen name, "Bic Fine Point," for this column.

Many of you, I'm sure have heard this language while passing a rancher moving cattle down the road and wondered what it meant. Or even if you didn't wonder what it meant, I'm sure you were awestruck by the sound of these mostly one-syllable words.

Each word listed below basically means the same thing when a rancher is speaking to a cow — "move your tail" — but with a slightly different emphasis.

"Yaw" is the starting word and simply means move your tail.

"Hup" means if you don't move your tail, I'm going to get mad.

"Whu" means I'm tired of saying Yaw and Hup.

"Yip" means maybe if I sound like a dog you will move a little faster.

"Git" means I just realized how silly I sound saying Yaw," "Hup," "Whu" and "Yip" so I will resort to a more normal sounding word (Get) even if I don't know how to say it properly.

A few rules to keep in mind: You have to start with Yaw, because it is the hardest to say and after a few miles of repeating "Hup," "Whu," "Yip" and "Git" you'll find that you no longer have the ability to form your mouth in the "Yaw" shape and will have missed the opportunity to say it. Each word is to be repeated several hundred times before moving on to the next. "Git" will also work for your stock dog when he runs in front of the cattle and chases them back in the opposite direction you want them to go.

Each word needs to be said with a certain amount of force and it's best to practice them for several days before actually trying them out on cows. If said incorrectly or too timidly the cows will just turn and laugh at you. (If in doubt about the proper enunciation you can always ask a seasoned rancher to give you cow-herding voice lessons, but be prepared to spend several hours, as he will undoubtedly take this opportunity to tell you everything else he knows about cows as well.)

And finally, warm up your vocal cords by yelling at your spouse, children or whoever else is planning on helping you herd the cows before you begin. This will also help set the mood for the day and give them the extra encouragement they will need to be forceful with the cows.

Another important note for herding cattle is that if you are a rancher's wife, be prepared to sit for long hours at a time blocking intersections while waiting for the herd to be moved by.

On my way to town the other day my good friend Shelly was engaged in this activity when I stopped to visit with her. She, like most all ranch wives, was told to be at this particular intersection at a precise time, not a moment later or it could foul up the entire operation.

Someone less experienced with this road blocking activity would have been there right on time and eagerly watching down the road for cattle, but Shelly and I knew it would be some time before we saw *anything* coming down the road, much less cattle.

Having had years of experience with this, and knowing that waiting for ranchers to bring cattle down the road is similar to waiting for rain in a drought, she was also prepared with a huge cup of coffee and some reading material. You might also want to consider towing along a porta-potty for just such an occasion.

But if your rancher-husband had the foresight to warm up his vocal cords by yelling at you before the cattle herding adventure began, you would have plenty to consider during your long intersection-blocking wait and reading material will not be necessary.

Little Pop N' Fresh

S ometimes dogs can be your best friends, and then sometimes they can eat your rolls...

I have a Dachshund, more commonly referred to by her scientific genus, "wiener doggie," that can be the sweetest, cutest, lovingest little critter — until her stomach gets in the way of her good sense. Then "Skippy" becomes a garbage hound willing to eat anything and everything that has the unfortunate fate of crossing her path. Actually it doesn't even have to cross her path — if need be she will go out of her way to hunt it down.

For years I have made homemade rolls and set the dough on the fireplace hearth to rise. For years Skippy has completely ignored the rolls. Thus, for years I've managed to amaze and astound visitors with my bread-making prowess. But last weekend we were having company for lunch and I was pressed for time. So for the first time ever (well, O.K. not the first, but close enough) I decided to use Rhodes frozen dinner rolls.

I prepared the rolls according to the package directions by placing the frozen mounds in a greased pan and then put them on the fireplace hearth where after a couple of hours, they slowly thawed and began to rise. I went about preparing the rest of the meal, confident the rolls would be ready in time.

A little while later Skippy came into the kitchen, drank about a gallon of water from her dog dish and began to belch and gurgle like a clogged up sink drain.

"What's the matter girl?," I asked as she looked up at me with wagging tail and big brown innocent eyes. "Do you have an upset stomach?"

I reached down to give her a pat and she immediately flipped over on her back. This is not really unusual because she is always trying to coax some poor unsuspecting human into rubbing her belly, but what was unusual was her belly. It was distended and with each little slurple, gurgle and cackling noise that it made, her belly slowly bubbled up and down. It looked as though she had a pot of stew simmering under the surface and it was obvious she wasn't the least bit happy about it.

Puzzled, I picked her up and carried her off to the living room to sit down with her and further examine the situation. It was then I passed by the fireplace and noticed that in the pan, where my 15 neat little rolls in a row resided, there was nothing — not even a trace of their prior existence. The butter I used to grease the pan with was even licked clean from the sides and bottom.

I looked at Skippy, "Did you eat my rolls?," I asked. She wagged her tail. "No, seriously," I said, "Did you eat my rolls?" Again she made with the tail wagging response. It was obvious I wasn't going to get a confession out of her, but by the size of her tummy it was also obvious that she had eaten every last one of them, and this was no small feat for a 10-pound dog. If you stacked the 15 rolls up two high and two wide they would be larger than her entire body.

Skippy was a sorry sight as she paddled around the house with her full dough belly in tow staggering like a drunk from the sheer weight - either that or the yeast had started to ferment already.

After a while though she finally settled down on the couch to rest and about the same time our company arrived and we went about the business of eating dinner – minus the rolls.

In the meantime Skippy had been sleeping peacefully — or so we thought....

When it came time to leave, our guest retrieved his coat, which had been placed on the couch near Skippy and proceeded to put it on. He looked down the sleeve as he put his arm through and a look of total disgust came across his face.

"Yuk! What's that stuff all over my sleeve?" he asked. As it turns out Skippy had decided to hurl and, apparently not wanting to mess up our couch (I taught her well), let loose on his coat. Trying to add humor to the situation I mentioned that if it hadn't been for Skippy we would not have found out that partially digested yeast will still rise on a down coat. After all, this bit of information may come in handy some day....

Not getting the amused response I had hoped for, I washed his coat and bid farewell, and then I sat down on the couch with Skippy and began to rub her still tight and aching belly.

Puddin' Head, our black lab, not wanting to be left out, sat at my feet and I rubbed her belly with my foot. After several relaxing moments, Skippy had inched forward until her head was hanging over the edge of the couch and again, without any warning, let loose spewing the doughy concoction all over Puddin' Head's head.

Apparently thinking she had been slimed with some kind of toxic substance Puddin' yowled and jumped up from the floor and took off running. I finally caught up with her and through all of her whining and twisting around managed to get her head cleaned off.

Puddin' sulked around the house the rest of the evening acting dejected and under no circumstances would go near the couch, which she perceived as the source of her humiliating experience.

Skippy seemed a little unconcerned with her rude outburst all over Puddin's head and briefly looked up before letting the dough fly again. This time Puddin' ran for cover and I later found her upstairs hiding under the bed.

Needless to say, I spent the rest of the night cleaning up piles of rising dough, which Skippy considerately dispersed throughout the house, while contemplating why she hadn't ever eaten my rolls before.

Why now after years of setting them on the fireplace hearth had she decided suddenly to eat them? And then it dawned on me —it was my homemade rolls that she didn't like — apparently she is a dog of discriminating tastes and preferred the Rhodes dinner rolls.

I'm happy to say Skippy made a complete recovery, but for some reason now every time you offer her a little piece of bread, she turns her nose up in the air.

It's My Story And I'm Sticking To It

I decided the other day that I needed to get more exercise during these slow winter months, specifically something aerobic in nature.

I'm used to bending, stretching and lifting — heck I lose a potato chip on the floor about three times a day while sitting at my computer at work and exert a considerable amount of energy trying to locate it before the dog gets it. But I understand that doctors are now saying we need more exercise than just fishing Pringles out of the can to keep healthy. And when I asked my doctor if adding Cheetos to my daily regime would help, he said more hand to mouth movement would only strengthen my appetite.

But not one to give up easily, I asked, "What if several times a day, I jump up from my computer at work, run across the room, tackle Doyle and steal one of his doughnuts?" The doctor said that while this may be beneficial to Doyle, any exercise I gained by the physical aspect of stealing his doughnuts would be counteracted by eating the doughnut. Apparently doughnuts have a way of actually soaking up any energy expended and converting it to lard, flour and sugar.

So after exhausting all of the food-related options for exercise, several things came to mind as I mulled this over, but

I knew whatever it was it needed to be outside in the fresh air — it's a rancher kind of thing.

I contemplated tossing bales of hay, but quickly ruled that out because we have nowhere to toss them too. Hurdling fences was also disqualified because I wouldn't be able to afford new britches every day. And since I realized barnyard calisthenics would give the neighbors too much to laugh about and swimming in the cattle trough was just plain gross, I decided to starting jogging.

Besides, I talked it over with my husband, Mike, and he rationalized that it would be especially good for me because I would be in better shape this spring when he needs me to run out and flank a cow or chase down a sick calf — presuming of course that he would be too busy to do it himself as is usually the case.

Anyway, running on a ranch isn't much different than running in town except you have different landmarks. Instead of setting your sights to make it five blocks to the corner of Third and Birch before running out of gas, you see if you can make it to the edge of the big turd and ditch. And once you get past that hurdle, it's on to the stinking dead cow, which is really a good landmark to run to because you won't spend much time loitering there before hightailing it to the old machinery graveyard, uh... I mean the rancher's very important inventory of parts. You never know when you might need a valve or an axle from half of an old 1892 John Deere tractor body.

So once I got my route figured out, Mike agreed to go with me and reminded me several times that I may not even make it to the first landmark, but being the nice guy that he is he will wait for me at our designated stopping point until dark. But I shouldn't expect too much beyond that, because he needs his sleep and therefore will check back the next morning to make sure I made it okay.

Well, as it turns out he should have saved his breath, because I shot out of the yard gates and into the field similar to an Olympic runner off the block. With my face to the wind, I raced through the snow like a young heifer escaping into the neighbor's pasture. My feet were moving so fast they just barely touched the ground, past the first landmark, on to the second, the third and... what's that? Hold on a minute —

Mike's reading over my shoulder and wants to interject something here....

Well, it's my story and I can write whatever I want...besides, they won't know...okay, okay...so I didn't even make it to the stinking dead cow, but the big turd at the ditch is five miles away...okay three miles...what? only 30 yards. It sure seemed a lot farther...and what do you mean five times, I only fell down twice. The three times I fell trying to get out of the yard don't count.

Anyway, as I was saying, it was spectacular; I was in the zone, my legs were strong, my back never felt better and...what? No, I don't think we need to tell them that you had to go back and get the truck to haul me home. Gosh, they don't want to know every single detail! Oh yeah, let's be sure and tell them how you made it all the way to the end without stopping once — not.

Well, I can see that I am going to have to continue this story at another time, darn back seat writers anyway. Maybe next time I can tell you about how I single-handedly wrestled down a charging bull and saved...wait, you can't unplug my computer, stop that...haven't you heard of freedom of speech...?

From Whence Milk Comes

I was in the grocery store the other day and watched as a little boy climbed up the side of a shopping cart his mother was pushing so he could examine the loot it contained. In a singsong voice he named off the items, especially the ones he had an interest in, "Cocoa Puffs, Pudding Pops, tater chips..." And out of all of the things in the cart, there was one item that he wanted to know where it came from. He didn't want to know how crispy balls of chocolate cereal were formed or how pudding could get on a stick; he wanted to know specifically where milk comes from.

The mother, not missing a beat, quickly responded as she threw a sack of artichokes in the cart and pointed in a far off direction saying, "It comes from over there in the dairy case." Completely satisfied with her answer the boy went back to the task at hand, "pasghetti, hangaburger....."

This little incident got me to thinking that maybe there are a lot of folks out there who think milk originates in the supermarket and are unaware of the role cows play in producing their dairy products. I also realized that cows very seldom get the recognition they deserve for performing this invaluable service.

So without further adieu, here is a list of popular dairy products and where they originate:

- Buttermilk – comes from cows that are constantly moving, churning and shaking their moo thing.
- 2 percent milk – comes from cows that aren't giving their "all" (100 percent).
- 1 percent milk – comes from cows that aren't giving diddley squat.
- Fat Free Milk – comes from health conscious cows that watch their cholesterol.
- Sour Cream – comes from cows that have gone bad.
- Powdered Milk – comes from cows raised in the desert.
- Lactose Free Milk – comes from cows that don't have any toes.
- Evaporated Milk – comes from cows that can't figure out where the milk went.
- Chocolate Milk – comes from cows that are fed a diet rich in Hershey's Syrup.
- Aged Cheese – comes from elderly cows.
- Blue Cheese – comes from cows that hold their breath.
- Half and Half – comes from cows that give half of the milk to the farmer and keep half of it for themselves.
- Whipping Cream – comes from cows with disciplinary problems.
- Ice Cream – comes from cows when the weather dips below 10 degrees.
- Enriched Milk – comes from cows owned by wealthy ranchers.
- Milk Duds – come from non-producing cows.

So next time someone asks you where milk comes from you can tell them not only where it comes from, but which cows produce the various products.

The next time I went to the grocery store, I tried explaining all of this to another little boy and he just gave me a puzzled look and began to get upset and yell for his mother. So I finally conceded and told him that it comes from the refrigerator, and he seemed perfectly satisfied with that.

'Uneasy Rider' Appearing Live On The Outdoor Movie Channel

I like to ride motorcycles. There — I said it. I know ranchers are suppose to like riding horses, but I prefer the two-wheeled models that go when I say go and stop when I put on the brakes. A motorcycle won't turn around and bite you when you're not looking or kick you in the shins when you accidentally touch them the wrong way. And it won't leave piles of poo for you to step in.

And even though motorcycles are great to ride on the ranch herding cows and doing chores they are also a lot of fun to ride in the mountains. Whenever I get an opportunity I jump on my trusty mechanical steed and ride like the wind — or at least like a gentle breeze.

A couple of weeks ago I had such an opportunity when my husband, Mike, had to go to the mountains to check some irrigation ditches. We loaded up the four-wheeler and my motorcycle in the back of the pickup and drove to the area where the ditch trail begins, which also happens to be a small camping area where a group of people were staying.

I hadn't been on my motorcycle in awhile and was feeling a little excited and over-confident, so I thought I would put on a good show for the campers who were all standing around their campfire drinking beer and noshing on what appeared to be pork rinds.

After unloading them, I jumped on, kick-started it like a pro and revved all 100ccs. The campers seemed duly impressed...a 100cc sounds a lot bigger than it really is and I'm sure they were wondering how I could possibly handle all that power — and I was about to show them.

So I took off going from zero to 10 mph in oh...I'd say about two minutes, with all eyes on me. I zoomed up the trail, wind blowing in my hair and bugs hitting my teeth, yes bugs can hit your teeth at 10 mph, especially the slow ones, and I rounded the first corner, which converges on a little foot bridge over the ditch. Going so "fast," I wasn't able to straighten my front wheel out in time before it hit the bridge, which had a wooden edge that sticks up about two inches. The tire caught that edge, and the cycle went totally out of control flipping me over sideways.

I looked over at my now entranced audience and they stood and watched as I struggled to get out from under the bike and pick it up. A 100cc bike isn't that big, but it weighs more than I do so it was a chore for me to pick up. After contorting my body into inhuman-like positions, much like playing a game of Twister, I finally managed to get it upright. I hopped on hoping for a quick exit from this embarrassing situation and kicked the starter and nothing happened. I tried a few more times and still nothing happened.

By this time the campers had pulled up stools and were all seated in a semi-circle to get the best viewpoint. It was then I realized that after having spent the night in the woods, these poor people had gone an entire 24 hours without television and I was like the outdoor movie channel.

Not wanting them to think I didn't know what I was doing, I started fiddling with the choke and various other hoses and greasy gadgets. At one point I even dug out a screwdriver and poked it around a little just to show them that I was not completely without mechanical skills.

In the meantime Mike, who was about two miles ahead of me before he finally realized I hadn't brought up the rear, came back looking for me. As he pulled up, I was still poking around with the screwdriver and seriously considering getting out the hammer when he said, "What are you doing? Stop playing around, we've got work to do."

"It won't start," I said.

"And you think poking the gas cap with a screwdriver is going to help?" he asked.

Not wanting to lose my credibility with my audience I said, "I'm checking the molecular activity of the gaseous fumes for conductivity to the transmission thereby establishing a solid contact with the errrr ahhh... catalytic converter!"

He just gave me a long sideways look, carefully considered the source of that string of gibberish for a moment, and weighed his next sentence against his desire to sleep on the couch that night. Then he said, "Here let me try." He climbed on kicked it once and it started right up.

"It was just flooded," he said. "What did you do dump it or something?" he asked half kidding.

I just gave him an airy laugh that may have in some way shape or form led him to believe that he was so far off base that it was funny — it obviously wasn't my intent though — I would have told him what really happened had he taken the time to question me for at least 10 minutes.

So once again I took off, this time a little more carefully from zero to about 6 mph in less than three minutes. I got a little ways down the trail and looked back at the campers who nonchalantly stood up, shrugged and once again began drinking beer and noshing pork rinds as if to say, "Nothing here to see folks, it's all over, move along."

But I didn't just leave them high and dry; I ended up providing them with more entertainment later on. Once we had gone several miles we reached a point where the ditch trail became too narrow for the four-wheeler to continue. So I took the 4-wheeler and headed back to the main road and Mike continued on the cycle. I was to get the pickup and meet him on the other side of the nearby reservoir.

It seemed like a perfectly fine plan until I got about halfway to the pickup and realized that I had never loaded a four-wheeler into the back of anything before. But how hard could it be?

Once at the pickup I pulled the ramp out and placed one end on the ground and the other on the tailgate. It's a one-ton pickup and about three feet off the ground so the ramp wasn't as horizontal as I would have liked, but I jumped on the four-wheeler and proceeded to climb up the ramp – several times. Every time I would get the front wheels on the ramp, it would flip up on one side and appear unsteady. So I backed up several times and tried to line the four-wheeler up better, but it didn't seem to help.

By this time my audience had turned their chairs to watch this HBO special and I was getting quite exasperated. I finally decided the worst that could happen if the ramp didn't stay in place was that the four-wheeler would simply fall down to the ground, so I mustered up my courage and gave it some gas. I kept climbing up the ramp even though it seemed wobbly and unstable until I finally made it into the back of the pickup. I now know that feeling of conquering a seemingly insurmountable challenge that mountain climbers have when they reach the top of Mount Everest. If I had a flag, I would have placed it in the fender well of the pickup.

Now all that was left was to get in the pickup and drive to our rendezvous point. I jumped in, turned the ignition....and nothing happened. I tried again and again and still nothing happened. The campers were obviously intrigued by this new turn of events because they had moved their movie seats a little closer. They were also beginning to get audio as I spouted words of "encouragement" to the piece of @!#$ pickup.

I decided poking around with a screwdriver this time wouldn't do any good and contemplated asking one of the campers for help, but they were pretty content to just watch. So I decided my only recourse was to get back on the four-wheeler and drive all the way to the backside of the reservoir on it. It wouldn't have bothered me so bad, but the thought of backing the four-wheeler out of the pickup wasn't something I was looking forward to. I reasoned that if it was so hard to get it in there, getting it out would really be a bugger.

So I finally decided I had no other options and reluctantly pulled the pickup keys out of the ignition and as I opened the door I happened to glance down at the floor. Wait, what's this? There's an extra pedal down there... Now, in my defense, my pickup is an automatic and I hardly ever drive Mike's and I did at least remember it was a diesel and to wait for the glow plug to light up every time I tried to start it...

although I have no idea what that's for or what good it does, but men in particular seem to think it's pretty darned important.

Not wanting to let my audience know that I forgot to push in the clutch and disappoint them — I'm sure up until this point that they had been pretty amazed by the feats I had accomplished this day — I leaned over and fiddled around under the dash for a few moments as if to "hot wire" the pickup as I've seen actors do on T.V shows before, pushed in the clutch, turned the ignition (glow plug be damned) and fired that baby right up.

As I drove out of the campsite I looked in my rearview mirror and the campers had gone back to standing around the fire and drinking their beer. But I was comforted by the knowledge that I had at least provided entertainment for their otherwise dreary day.

Fetching Parts Is For
The Dogs

Tractors, hay rakes, balers, combines, trucks and other types of ranching machines are each made up of hundreds of parts. And somewhere, at some time, there was an unwritten law made that says it is the ranch wife's responsibility to fetch those parts whenever one fails.

Taking into consideration that most of us don't know an alternator from a carburetor, one might wonder why we have been given this obligation. You would think that after sending their wives on dozens of unsuccessful trips to the parts store, husbands would see that there is a problem with this fetching system.

The rancher's logic, though, is that he can teach his dog to retrieve an object that is thrown, so surely a wife that is given a part can go fetch one that looks exactly the same.

But in the ranch wife's defense, the dogs actually have it easier. The object that a dog is asked to retrieve is seldom slathered with grease, dripping with oil and unrecognizable. There are not 14 different places that a dog has to look for an object, and they know the general direction in which it was thrown.

For a dog, retrieving an object is not a half-day event. If he can't find it, a dog gives up in 15 minutes, and the rancher pets the dog's head and says, "That's okay boy, better luck next time." But, if after a couple of hours, the ranch wife returns from town and says she can't find the part, the rancher pats her hand and says, "Don't worry about dinner Honey, I can wait until you get back from Boise, it will only take you four or five hours and they'll have the part — you can make me something to eat when you get home."

And for some reason, at this point if a wife begins to complain, ownership of everything on the ranch is magically transferred to her. He says, "I really need this part so I can hook 'your' tractor up to 'your' hay wagon and feed 'your' cows so I can make 'you' some money."

So drunken with the power of ownership and the promise of money, we pick up the greasy blob of cold steel again and willing to give it another try ask our husbands, "Where does this part go? What is it called? And do I need to know the make, model and year of the tractor?"

He inevitably replies, "Nah, don't worry about it. People at those parts stores are professionals. One look at that part and they will know exactly what you need. In fact, they don't like it if you give them too much information, makes them look stupid." Which loosely translates into, "I don't feel like looking that stuff up and I don't remember what it's called."

So after the two-hour drive to Boise and another hour of trying to locate the part store, which by the way the husband could not remember the name of either, (he could only remember that the billboard next to it had a picture of a bikini-clad woman and that there was a Victoria's Secret store across the street) the wife finds the store and takes the part up to the counter.

The first words out of the parts store clerk's mouth are, "What is this thing and what make, model and year is the machine it came from?"

Remembering what the husband had said, it becomes obvious the clerk doesn't mind looking stupid. And in turn, we don't win very many IQ points ourselves in the process, while spitting out something like, "Well, I'm not sure... I know it came off of a tractor, I think it was a green one and wherever it goes it apparently needs a lot of grease in order to run correctly. My husband said he needed it to be able to feed my cows, if that helps."

The clerk always gives the wife that "look," which roughly translates into, "He should have sent the dog."

So after another hour of watching the clerk thumb through catalogs of parts and occasionally running to the storeroom to compare it to another part, he presents three possibilities. Having been in this situation many times before, we wisely take all three to avoid having to make a return trip.

Three hours later, you return home with the parts, which with all of the trouble it took you to get them, are beginning to resemble the Holy Grail, and you gingerly place them in your husband's hands.

The first words out of his mouth are, "I only needed one, how come you got three? And boy, these things are expensive, I would of jerry-rigged something together and made it work if I would of known they cost this much."

With that he heads for the shop and says, "You start dinner and I'll go install this in *my* tractor, so I can hook up *my* hay wagon to feed *my* cows and make *me* some money."

And once again the power of ownership has shifted...

The Diarrhea Debate

R anchers have a tendency to think that everyone automatically knows what they are talking about. After all doesn't everyone think in cow terms?

I was in the grocery store the other day and decided to go to the pharmacy section and check out the diarrhea medicine. We had a sick calf at home that just didn't seem to be responding to the standard treatment.

As I was browsing the different types and reading labels trying to figure out the best brand, one of the store pharmacists came over and offered his assistance. I decided to take this opportunity to ask an expert which medicine would be best, or if there was any difference in the brands.

So he said, "Tell me what the symptoms are and perhaps I can tell you which type would work better."

I said, "You know, the usual—severe diarrhea with head hanging to the ground and droopy-eyes."

He asked, "Does he have a fever?"

"Well I didn't want to go to the trouble of taking his temperature, but I would say he does by the looks of the blistering on his nose," I said.

"Wow, he must be a pretty sick little fella," he said. "How severe is the diarrhea?"

"Well," I said, "He's pretty much squirting it out all the time, especially when he's out running around through the grass."

"I see," said the pharmacist as he ponders this information for a moment. "But," he said, "Do you think you should be letting him run around outside in the grass when he's so sick?"

"There's not much I can do about that," I said. "He's awfully hard to catch and I certainly don't want him in the house, he's too big and would make too big of a mess."

"How old is he?" asks the pharmacist.

"He's about 4 months old," I replied.

"Good grief," he said, a little annoyed by the sound of the situation. "He's only 4 months old, has severe diarrhea, a fever and you're letting him run around outside in the grass! You need to take him to a doctor right away."

"Look," I said, "we have so many that if I took them to the doctor every time they got sick, we'd go broke. I was just hoping you could tell me what brand and how much to give him. I've been giving him a quarter of a cup of this brand," I said pointing to the pink bottle, "in an electrolyte mix and drenching him with a tube, does that sound about right or do you have any ideas of what might work better? He's not recovering as fast as I would like."

The pharmacist shook his head, picked up a bottle and rather sternly said, "First of all, a 4 month-old should only get 1/2 a teaspoon, if any. He's probably only weighs about 20 pounds doesn't he?"

Not sure what side of the planet this joker was born on, I told him, "I said he was sick, I didn't say he was dead, he weighs about 350 pounds."

"O.K., now I've heard everything," he said. "You're trying to tell me that you have a 4 month-old that weighs 350 pounds!"

"I know, he should weigh a little more than that for his age, but like I've been telling you—he's sick," I said. "He's probably losing somewhere around five pounds a day. He's starting to get pretty dehydrated too. Do you think I should I.V. him with some distilled water and baking soda?"

"This is getting ridiculous," said the pharmacist. "You have a 4-month old son that weighs 350 pounds, runs around in the grass with diarrhea and a fever, you won't let him in the house because he would make too big of a mess and you won't take him to the doctor because you have too many other kids. Furthermore you are sticking a tube down his throat to give him a gosh awful amount of medicine. And no, under no circumstances should you attempt to give him an I.V.! Do you have any idea how bad all of this sounds?"

"Well, when you put it like that it does sound pretty bad," I said. "But I don't have a 4 month-old son, I have a 4 month-old calf."

This is one of those defining moments when it took all of my will power not to follow my real teenage son's vocabulary and say "Duuuuuh!"

The pharmacist just shook his head and walked off, muttering something about not being a "dang" veterinarian. As best I could tell our conversation was over and I still didn't find out which diarrhea brand four out of five pharmacists prefer.

To Market, To Market To Sell Fat Calves

It has been said that you can always count on two things — death and taxes. For ranchers there are three things — death, taxes and the price of calves will go down the day you sell them. Even if the price has remained at a steady high for three months, the day you pull into the sale yard with a truckload of calves will be the day the market takes a dive.

And to make things worse, fat little calves that have been at their prime for weeks will go off feed and take laxatives the day before the sale, resulting in 20-pound loss per head. And those young strong healthy calves that weren't in on the weight-loss plot will act sick in the sale ring with heads hanging low and ears drooping. Some will even fake a limp — you can always spot the fakers — they will get halfway through the ring and change legs, but so subtly that buyers won't notice.

And if that weren't bad enough the cows add to the pandemonium by running the calves around the fields for hours while you try to herd them into the corrals to take to the sale. This activity results in another 20-pound reduction — both on the calves and us.

The nice gentle cows that would normally walk into the corrals with little or no prompting go ballistic. It's like the minute you step into the field one cow yells, "Run for your lives," and everyone takes off at a gallop. They don't know where they're going — they just go.

And about the time you think you have the herd rounded up and going in the right direction, two or three will bolt and make a run for it and the whole ordeal starts over again.

Now why would the cows do this? We plow through three feet of snow (up hill) in the winter months with minus 10-degree weather nipping our noses to feed them, and swelter in 100-degree heat, working 15-hour days during the summer months to produce their hay. We care for them when they are sick or in pain. We take care of their babies, if for some reason they choose not to take on this responsibility, and we shell out thousands of dollars for their upkeep and maintenance.

You would think that after all of this, they would be grateful enough to quietly and calmly give up their calves so that we could sell them and get some money for all of our hard work. But noooooooooooooo! They try and hang on to those little buggers until we have to pry them out of their cloven hooves.

The baffling thing is that as I watch the cows out in the pastures this time of year, after months of producing milk for the little suckers, you can tell that they are really tired of them.

The cows actually start exhibiting signs of apathy toward their calves long before the weaning takes place and will no longer even respond to one that is bawling. When the calves were younger, all they had to do was open their mouth and act like they were about to bawl and ten cows would come running to see what was wrong. Now, when a calf bawls, they look around guiltily at each other as if to say, "I'm not going, are you going? No, I'm not going, maybe she will go..."

I've also seen the cows kicking at the calves during feeding time. They try to cover up this activity by acting like they are trying to get at a fly or an itch or coughing at the same time they kick. But once in awhile you'll see a cow belt a calf square on the head and there was no mistaking her intent. She then looks around to see if anyone was watching, but the other cows purposely turn the other way and act like nothing happened. And often, after such an incident, the other cows will approach her and before long she has them all lined up practicing kickboxing.

Cows that normally wanted their calves by their sides in the earlier weeks are also now sending them off to play in remote corners of the field. Some cows even go so far as to hide from the calves in discreet places such as your flowerbeds and gardens thinking the calves would never look there.

So it's hard to understand why the cows put up such a fuss when it comes time to wean the calves and take them to market. But I do have a theory — it's not that the cows particularly want them — it's just that they don't want us to have them.

Rancher's Wisdom

With age comes wisdom and ranchers are no exception. If you are just starting out in the ranching business, seek the advice of an older, more experienced rancher — they are always eager to give you hands-on training. Spend some time with them and by paying close attention and doing exactly as they say, both of you will undoubtedly profit from the encounter. Here are some examples of the comments you may hear in different situations as these seasoned professionals teach lessons in ranching.

"Changing sprinklers is one of the most enjoyable parts of being a rancher, especially hand lines. It's so much fun, I generally like to do it myself. I guess I could let you change them though, since you need the experience — in fact I'll tell you what, since you're such a nice guy I'll let you change them for the entire season — no sense in me being greedy."

"Run down the cattle chute and stick your head in the head catch so I can show you how it works...Yep looks like it's working fine. Don't worry, a little WD-40 and a crow bar and we'll have your head out of there in no time. In the mean time, I'd better bring you some dinner just in case, and maybe a blanket for tonight, but I guarantee we'll have you out of there by tomorrow morning for sure."

"Bulls? Naaah they're really gentle. You can just walk up to them and scratch their ears. Go ahead, try it and while you're at it slip this rope around his neck and see if you can give him this vaccine. Just stick the four-inch needle into his hindquarters and squeeze the trigger. Don't worry, their hide is so thick he won't feel a thing. I'd go with you but I got my new boots on. Come to think of it I better stand way over here just to make sure I don't get them dirty."

"No sense in wasting time to go get tools. Anyone can fix a fence with wire stretchers and a hammer, but it takes real skill to get the job done with a rock. Let me demonstrate...No, I didn't hurt myself, I just noticed the grass was a little dry and I wanted to show you the rancher's rain dance. You just place your flattened thumb between your knees and hop up and down while chanting $!!*!#@$!*."

"If you're gonna be a rancher you gotta have a good horse. I've got one I can sell you for next to nothing. He belongs to my wife but for some reason she never wants to ride Ol' Tornado, guess she just doesn't have time. Give him a try — he's plumb gentle. He'll stop that bucking as soon as you get on. I would show you but my arthritis is acting up today."

"I don't know what fool told you that calves are hard to ear tag while their mothers are around, it's easy. I've got three calves out there right now that need tags. Go on out there and see for yourself. No, don't worry, those mother cows are just playing with you, pretty soon they'll get tired of chasing you and then you can catch their calves. That's it, son, bring your knees up high when you run."

"See, this is the way the water rights work. My papers say I've got 1914 water rights and my neighbor Jim Bob McKracken has 1892 water rights. Since I have the newest claim, I get water first. Yours are 1876 so I'm afraid you're gonna be the last to get water, son — that's a dirty shame."

"You have to develop a good relationship with the local parts store. In fact, why don't you start right now by running to town, I've got just a few things on this list here. No, it's not unusual to need 50 parts just for the baler. Oh, and you may have to go to Boise to get some of them, it's only an extra 100 miles, but don't worry I don't mind waiting — glad to help you out."

"You need to get yourself at least three cow dogs. They don't have to know anything about cattle, their main job is advertising. When they ride around in the back of your pickup people will know that you're a rancher — saves you from having to say anything."

"You'll find that shovel handles don't work, they break off every time you take your four-wheeler through a gate. So instead you need to learn how to use a shovel blade without the handle — nothing to it. You just need to know what you're doing, let me demonstrate...no everything's fine, just a little more of that rain dance, son."

The Backside Of Ranching

F armers and ranchers suffer from all kinds of ailments, aches and pains just like the rest of the population, but there are a few that are unique to the industry.

In fact with all of the fieldwork going on this time of year, the most common complaint afflicting them now is seldom talked about — as it is a rather "tender" one. You might even say it is a problem they would like to put "behind" them as soon as possible.

I know because I too have suffered from the annoying and often painful effects of "Tractor Bottomitis" (TB). Those who rake hay, bale, harrow, plow, combine and seed — basically any work that involves a tractor — are all at risk of contacting TB.

The progression of TB is gradual and it may take up to two 12-hour days of sitting in a tractor seat before the symptoms of discomfort and accompanying rash are apparent.

People with TB are easy to spot. They are prone to restless squirming and shifting while seated in a chair, and it is often confused with another well know affliction — "Ants In Your Pants."

You may also find that those with TB will insist on standing in the back at church through the entire two-hour service, take inflatable plastic donuts to the movies and, out of character, will gladly offer their chair to anyone who arrives, even the neighbor's cat.

They often resort to childish behavior, yelling things like, "I get dubs on the recliner," and "That tube of Ben Gay has my name on it," as they race the family to the house.

TB has become such a problem that a group of protesters called "Ranchers Everywhere Against Rashes" (REAR) has been formed to combat the effects of TB and are lobbying to make adjustable comfort cushions a mandatory feature in public places. Eating establishments, for example, could offer cushioned sections for those with TB and other afflictions, and non-cushioned sections for those who prefer to be seated on the standard rock-hard surfaces.

I.C. Buns, a spokesperson for the REAR, says bumper stickers are beginning to crop up everywhere with catchy sayings such as "Support Your Local REAR," "A New REAR For The People" and "REAR Fights For Your Comfort."

Buns says REAR is considering the possibility of converging with another organization called CHEEKS, "Cowboys Have Earned Every Known Saddle-sore" to double their efforts.

"We at REAR believe that once we have established a working relationship with CHEEKS, we will begin to see progress in our fight for mandatory cushions," said Buns.

CHEEKS had been lobbying for changes long before REAR came into the picture and has been trying to get a measure put on the ballots that will entitle saddle sore cowboys to Workman's Compensation benefits.

"It's just another hazard of the job," says CHEEKS Director Westward Ho. "We should be allowed to have the same type of benefits others in the workforce receive even if our injuries are not as visible as some."

If CHEEKS and REAR do form a partnership, Senator Wares Mymoney says they will be an emerging force to be reckoned with.

"The CHEEKS and REAR have been a great concern for us," says Mymoney. "But where do you draw the line? If we let this mandatory cushion rule go through, what's next, comfortable airplane seats? Frankly, I see no end in sight."

One problem with the merger of the two organizations is that CHEEKS has been, in part, funded by several well-known western movie actors. REAR on the other hand has been slighted in this department with their largest contributors being ranchers, most of whom haven't shown a profit in several years.

Buns says the main concern is that if the two organizations combine, would CHEEKS be willing to split funding right down the center in order to operate as a unit?

The most obvious problem as I see it, is that the mandatory cushion measures don't have much of a chance of even making it to the ballots because the government hasn't figured out a profitable way to tax the CHEEKS and REAR yet — but I suspect they are working on it!

Ranchers Are Thankful When...

T hanksgiving is traditionally a time for families and friends to gather together and count the many things that they have to be thankful for. This event can be a particularly heart-warming experience for ranchers as they have many things to be thankful for including the following.

Ranchers are thankful when:

• Their $500 stock dog doesn't stand in the gate they are trying to push cattle through.

• The neighbor's prize-winning bull jumps in their pasture with their cows during breeding season and stays a few weeks.

• Nobody notices they are using a little "extra" water during irrigation season.

• They don't make their wives mad enough to leave during the first five minutes of branding calves.

• They can find an irrigation boot for each foot and they don't have any leaks in them.

• They can get a glove out of the dog's mouth that has minimal slobber and few enough holes that it is still usable.

• There are still two or three good posts left in a half-mile section of fence.

• The cows decide to go into the corrals after only three galloping trips around the pasture instead of the customary five.

• They can find the duct tape — because without it, the tractor won't run.

• They have kids old enough to do chores so they don't have to any more. (This blessing contributed by my son, Jake)

• They don't get bucked off the four-wheeler as often as they do the horse and the machine seldom turns up lame.

• They finally remember where they put their shovel and it's still there after all those years.

• Someone in town tells them the smell of cow poop on their boots is undetectable even though it can be seen and is leaving a trail.

• They can still use the Come-Along winch to move heavy items when the hitch in their get-along is acting up.

• At least one out of 20 heifers immediately wants its calf and isn't leaping over fences into the next county.

• They look around and realize no one saw their imitation of Captain Hook performed while loading hay on the wagon with the hay hooks.

• They pluck the last of the chicken feathers from between the dog's teeth just before the wife gets home to find out what "really" happened to her Rhode Island Red.

But most of all ranchers are thankful for the opportunity to live and love and share their lives with friends and family in the countryside — and when they remember to remove the giblets from the turkey *before* cooking it.

A Martha Stewart
Thanksgiving

T hanksgiving began like any other holiday, full of hope and enthusiasm that the day would be filled with harmony and laughter. I envisioned myself in my moo-cow apron greeting our guests as they arrive with a spring in my step and a smile on my face. The fireplace would be softly glowing, the turkey would be done to perfection and everyone would be in awe as they sat around my exquisitely decorated table — not!

My idealistic little bubble burst about 7 a.m., when Martha Stewart entered the picture. I'm not saying that Martha ruined my Thanksgiving, but she certainly didn't help matters any.

To explain how the events transpired, I began working full time at *The Record-Courier* this summer and consequently my husband, Mike, who is a rancher and is able to spend more time at home, began taking over a lot of the cooking responsibilities. As with anything else he does, he can't just do a so-so job to get by, he has to research, study, and completely engulf himself in a project including cooking.

In the past few months, I have sampled everything from apple pear compost to cow cow yuk. His cooking really began to improve when he discovered the Food Network on T.V. a few weeks ago. With the help of Emeril, Wolf Gang Puck and yes, Martha Stewart, he has been making absolutely delicious meals every night.

Now you may ask, how could this possibly be a problem? Well, up until Thanksgiving morning, it wasn't. I woke up that morning singing and dancing my way to the kitchen as usual.....okay so I'm not a morning person, I dragged my weary carcass into the kitchen and began to prepare the turkey.

Normally Mike has learned not to talk to me for the first 30 minutes upon rising, because even though I'm up and mobile, nothing good comes out of my mouth until I'm fully awake. But for some reason he broke that unspoken rule and said, "Are you sure you should be rinsing out the turkey cavity like that? Martha Stewart says there are a lot of good juices in there that you want to keep."

Now, I really try hard to suppress my innate morning crankiness, but come on, Martha Stewart. So between clenched teeth, I not so politely said, "I've been cooking turkeys for just as many years as Martha Stewart and nobody's complained yet!"

Quieted for a little while, he continued to observe my unrefined culinary prowess, as I not so gently, due to my agitated state, slapped the bird around the sink. I almost lost the turkey at one point when it slipped out of my hands and scurried across the kitchen counter. I saved it from landing on the floor with a hip-to-cabinet move, at which point Mike cried, "Fowl, unnecessary roughness!" It would have been funny, if he hadn't followed up with, "I've never seen Martha handle a bird that way, I don't think it's a good thing."

I don't have anything personal against the Susie Homemaker of T.V. land, but she was really beginning to get on my nerves as Mike continued to offer Martha's words of wisdom.

The final blow came when I was preparing the stuffing and Mike said, "Martha says you should stuff the neck cavity first and cook the turkey with the breast side down but that's okay, don't feel bad, because everyone usually does it wrong."

I picked up the turkey, shoved it at Mike and said, "Here, you and Martha can stuff it!" At that point I decided that I wanted nothing more to do with the bird, and with an air of satisfaction, I stomped out of the kitchen. Fortunately for the guests, Mike did stuff it and cook it, and the turkey turned out beautifully. By the time dinner was ready, I was beginning to wonder if maybe Martha did know something, but I wasn't about to admit it.

We had one other run in with Martha during the day when it came time to make the gravy. I've always made gravy with flour, but Mike said, "Martha recommends making it with corn starch."

I replied, "Well if you know how to make gravy Martha's way go right ahead." So he proceeded to get out the ingredients, looked at the pan, looked at me and then made a dive for the cookbook. Need I say which one — "Cooking With Martha." Upon examining her recipe for gravy, he asked me to read it because he didn't understand one of the directions. "I replied, "Don't ask me, I make gravy with flour."

Then after about ten minutes of discussing the virtues of using cornstarch or flour, butter or pan drippings, and whether or not Martha knows diddily squat, our good friend Doug, who was joining us for dinner, tired of our gravy exchanges. "Good grief, I'll show you both how to make the gravy," he said. And he did — some of the best gravy we have ever had.

After dinner, and the guests had departed, Mike and I recounted the day's events and decided that we may be on to something here. Next year we could wait until Doug came over to start the turkey and get him to cook that as well! Mike says, "Heck, I'll bet we could pick an argument about the yams and mashed potatoes too!" As Martha would say, this could be "a good thing."

All references to Martha Stewart were meant solely for entertainment purposes and are in no way a reflection of the real Martha Stewart, who is a really sensational cook who knows everything – not!

It's All About Power...

B uying Christmas presents for a rancher is not much different than buying presents for the general population of men. They basically have the same wants — anything with power: tools, machinery, guns and particularly anything with words like "turbo," "4x4, " "high-speed" or "super size" written on it.

The problem comes in when you decide to try and buy them something that you think they "need" instead of "want."

If the manufacturer of "Levis" Jeans could include something on the label that said, "Turbo reinforced seams with super size 4x4 seat and high-speed zipper," the gift-giving problem would be solved and wives could finally throw away all of their husband's old worn out jeans.

Or those scuffed up leaky work boots could be easily replaced with a pair of "Rugged 4x4 boots with super size turbo power soles made from an Angus certified steer chased down at 170 mph and shot with a 7mm carbine rifle."

But, since companies haven't utilized that type of marketing strategy yet, resourceful ranch wives have come up with a few ways to sneak in some things that their husbands need while still buying them what they want. When selecting these items pay close attention to the key words written on the box, which will ultimately determine whether or not they will be happy with their gift.

• You can get away with buying a rancher a coat, as long as you accessorize it with a "high speed" cordless power drill.

• You can wrap a scarf and gloves around the legs of a "super size" table saw and use a knit hat as a blade cover.

• A cowboy hat can be concealed as a "turbo" router cover.

• Several pairs of socks can be slipped over the barrel of a "lever action" rifle to protect it from scratches.

• The legs on a pair of jeans can be tied at the ends and filled with "high speed trajectory" 12-gauge shot shells.

• A flannel shirt can be folded and tied as a bow around several "4x4" pieces of "rough cut" lumber.

• Insulated bib overalls can be disguised as a tool apron if you insert items in the pockets such as a "mega" tape measure, "heavy duty" "rip" hammer, "super torque" ratchet set and a "28-inch" "super oscillating" "power grip" chainsaw capable of sawing down trees in a single pass.

The only thing to remember is that a few days after Christmas you have to secretly slip the hats, gloves, coat, jeans, etc. into his closet and dresser without his knowledge, otherwise he will never use them for their intended purpose. And then you have to practice the "look." That would be the dumbfounded look you need to give him when he asks if you know what happened to his router cover, table saw accessories, rifle sleeves, tool apron and shot shell holder.

However, there are some gifts that you can get a rancher year after year because they never grow tired of them, and they can never have too many because they lose or break one a month on the average: whips, hotshots, grease guns, vaccine syringes, fence stretchers, fencing pliers, shovels and pickup tail gates.

And if all else fails, and he doesn't like the selection of gifts you purchased, he can always borrow yours, because it's almost certain that he will buy you that skill saw and shotgun that he claims "you've always wanted."

Laughing Cows And Billiard Woes

The cows were planning something big for Christmas this year. They huddled and chewed their cud for weeks as they discussed what fun antics they could do to make our Christmas more "memorable." At one point I even heard them whispering something about taking off for Union County. From what I could gather they had heard that there was no snow and cows there still had some good grass available.

Two days before the holiday, they were milling around the pasture behind the house — where we have a large picture window they can see in — firming up their plans. And as they watched us, we could see the excitement in their eyes. They were like youngsters on the first day of summer vacation, bucking and kicking up their heels in anticipation of some serious holiday escapades.

But as they continued to take turns watching us, they began to laugh (as only cows can) and they tee-heed and chortled as they crowed and pushed each other out of the way to get a better view. And the harder they laughed, somehow their plans became less important as they saw how easily we could mess up our own holidays without their help.

We had decided on a family gift this year, or as my husband, Mike, puts it, I had decided and he went along with it because he's such a nice guy. But, in my defense, who would have guessed that a pool table could come "ready to assemble" and be in so many pieces? The sales person said it would arrive in three boxes, one with the legs, one with the top and one with the side rails. So naturally I figured it would be a piece of cake — we'd stand up the legs, slap on the top and attach the rails – how much easier could it be?

As it turns out it could have been a whole helluva lot easier. The "legs" were a pile of boards with bolts, nuts and screws, the slate top came in three pieces with the felt top neatly rolled up and a can of glue beside it, and the rails were in several pieces with the ball holes (or now as bonafide pool experts what we refer to as "billiard pockets") unattached. And if that weren't bad enough, the entire frame had to be built — but of course, all of the parts and instructions needed were included in your handy dandy pool table kit.

Our son Jake had gotten a head start on the project by unpacking all of the materials and carefully laying them out around the room like pieces of a giant jigsaw puzzle. After examining all of the parts, we were taken aback at how much needed to be done, but we still figured with three of us, we could complete the project in less than the six hours the manual said it took the "average" person to complete. Well, we learned something very important during the course of the two days it took us to complete it — apparently we're not "average."

We also learned that the instruction manual was not designed for us, the "un-average people," to comprehend. For instance the first problem we encountered was when it instructed us to attach panel number one to the "right side." Well, if you stand at one end of the table, the "right side" is different than if you stand at the other end of the table. So how do you determine which right side is the right, right side?

Fortunately, (depending on which way you look at it) Mike completely took over at this point and began orchestrating the project. He circled the table several times with his trusty tape measure, held up the panel and tried fitting it on both sides, and finally announced as he deftly pulled out his cordless power drill, "This is the 'right side.'"

Jake and I were in awe of his uncanny ability to determine which was the correct side, even though it eventually had to be taken down and moved to the "other" right side.

About halfway through the project, and into our second day of assembly, I was browsing through the vast array of hardware looking for a 3/4-inch hex bolt with a split lock steel washer and a standard coarse-threaded nut, when I discovered a little white box. Instead of just looking inside, of course, I had to hold it up and ask the perplexing question, as most people do, "What's this?"

"I dunno," said Jake. "It came with the pool table kit so it must be something that goes on it." After rotating the little box around and examining all sides of it, looking for writing or other telltale signs of what might be inside, and making several attempts at guessing what it might be, Mike slowly and deliberately said, "Just open the damn box."

Dragging the suspense on just a little bit longer, until I could sense that Mike and Jake were about ready to pummel me with a cue stick, I opened the box...and there inside was the Holy Grail of all pool table kits...the pot of gold at the end of the slate top rainbow...a step-by-step instructional video on how to assemble the pool table. And I had found it. I basked in the glory of the moment...enjoying what it felt like to be a hero and save the day... until Jake said, "Oh yeah, I knew that was in there, I thought you were looking at something else."

After fast forwarding the tape past all of the things we had assembled incorrectly, but were too late to change, we were able to finish the pool table in another six hours. So the instruction book wasn't entirely wrong — after two days of figuring things out and assembling half of the table — it really did only take only six hours to complete.

We had to use this reasoning in order to gain our "average" status again, and show the cows we could do it. Although by this time the cows had tired of laughing and had lost interest about 23 hours earlier — they were off plotting and planning another scheme for New Year's Day.

I'm Dreaming Of A Moo-less Christmas

T he cows are up to something... They've been sneaking around for two weeks plotting and making plans for Christmas. I know this because every time I go out to the corrals to feed or fill the water tanks, they are huddled together whispering moo stuff. When they see me coming, they break up and nonchalantly wander off chewing their cuds. I'm sure if they could stuff their hooves in their pockets and whistle, they would.

Last year they involved one of the bulls in their little Christmas morning escapade. They held the fence wires apart so Angus McNasty could sneak into the pen with them. We have three bulls, all named in accordance with their personalities, McNasty, McNerdy and McTurdy. But McNasty is always the one causing problems, so I'm sure that's why the girls chose him.

They somehow cajoled McNasty into using his head as a battering ram to knock down the gate to their pen, allowing them to escape into the pasture. Once in the pasture they had plans to run McNasty through the barbed wire fence near the highway and make their escape.

After knocking down the gate, McNasty was on an adrenaline high, which was escalated by the cheers and moos of the cows as they bucked and kicked behind him. Like a linebacker heading down the football field, he charged through the snow with the cows in tow.

It was a masterful plan and it would have worked if Mike hadn't looked out the window and saw the whole scheme unfold before his eyes. Before he could say, "What are those damn cows doing now," they were already halfway across the pasture. I hurriedly threw the turkey in the oven and we bolted out the door after the stampeding bovines.

Over the years Mike has managed to train me to run around the cows in different directions to herd them, eliminating the need for a good cow dog. He whistles to catch my attention and then points out the direction for me to run in. He also has hand motions to signal me to move back or come in close. If I'm too far out in the field to properly decipher his signals, then he jumps up and down and flaps his arms in all directions and that means to stop and just stand there. And if he yells, "Go back to the house, I can do it myself," that usually means I got mad and quit following his directions.

This particular morning took about three hours of running around the field until the cows finally gave up and allowed us to herd them back to the pen. By this time the mob had lost their enthusiasm and slowly made their way back with the exhausted McNasty bringing up the rear with his head hung low in defeat.

By the time we got the gate fixed and everyone situated, the turkey was well on its way to being done. We finished up the rest of the meal and our guests arrived just as the turkey was ready to be carved. We were all standing around the turkey oohing and awing at how good it looked when Mike cut into the bird revealing a big black burnt glob in the cavity. It was then I realized that the Butterball company hadn't forgotten to include the giblets — in my haste I had forgotten to take them out. I could almost hear the cows laughing outside and consoling McNasty — "It's okay McNasty, we may not have escaped, but we did manage to make her screw up the turkey."

That was just one Christmas that the cows tried to interfere with our yuletide fun. The year before that they escaped into the yard and when we all sat down for Christmas dinner, one of the cows edged up to the window and pressed her nose against the glass. When my mom turned to see what everyone was looking at, the sight of two huge nostrils, with a hairy face and beady little eyes nearly caused her to flip her plate off of the table.

One year the cows even went so far as to hire a hit man. Early Christmas morning they had him slide off the road in his pickup and knock down an entire section of fence. The cows made it out the opening and were jogging down the highway at a pretty good clip before we caught up with them.

The cows don't ever seem to be going anywhere in particular when they escape. I've heard Mike ask them before, "Where in the hell do you think you're going?" They just stare at him with that same blank look you get when you ask a teenager that question.

So given their past history, I know the cows are up to something — I guess we'll find out on Christmas morning. Happy Holidays.

'Twas A Night With More Cows

'T was the night before Christmas and all through the house,
Not a creature was stirring except for them damn cows;
The cows were all creeping by the house without care,
In hopes that they would wake up everyone there;

The guests were all nestled snug in their beds,
With visions of sleep dancing through their heads;
And Mike in his long johns and I in mine too,
Had just settled in for a night without moo;

When out in the yard there arouse such a clatter,
We sprang from our bed to see what was the matter;
Away to the porch we flew like a jet,
Threw open the door and immediately got wet;

The cows looked like beasts in the wind and the snow,
And had made the ground brown with poop down below;
Then, what to our dismayed eyes should appear,
Three bulls with six horses bringing up the rear;

Now McNasty, now McTurdy, and the rest of you damn
cows,
On you dang horses, stop pestering us now;
To the gate to the pasture, out of the yard we both call,
Now get away, get away, get away, all!

As Mike got madder his temper did rise,
He cursed at the cows, planning their demise;
So around the yard the cows they did run,
With the horses and bulls all having their fun;

And then, while chasing the cows, I heard Mike speak,
Go get the four-wheeler, I'm getting too weak;
As I ran to the barn to follow his request,
I noticed the chickens were all out of their nests;

They had ruffled their feathers from heads to their feet,
And were squawking and clucking and pecking their
beaks;
I herded them up and put them back in their quarters,
And took the four-wheeler continuing my orders;

Mike's eyes how they flared, as he looked at me weary,
His jaws were clenched tight and he didn't look merry;
"Where have you been and I want to know now,
Why weren't you here helping me chase these damn
cows?"

As I told him my story of chickens gone wild,
The tension in his forehead began to grow mild;
We jumped on the four-wheeler and continued our
chase,
After all of the cattle and horses we raced;

The cows when they ran, their udders jiggled,
Like a bowl full of jelly, they bounced and they wiggled;
The bulls were less funny and even looked mad,
As they dodged and darted until they knew they'd been
had;

The horses were easy, they wanted to be fed,

We lured one with hay, and haltered his head;
The others followed right down to gate,
Where we locked them in and sealed their fate.

Mike spoke not a word, but went straight to bed,
Where he fluffed up his pillow and laid down his head;
I too was tired and had almost fallen asleep,
When Mike abruptly sat up in a disarrayed heap;

"What was that," he said, "did you hear a moo?"
I sat up in bed and I began to listen too;
It started out softly and sounded far away,
But then it grew louder as they started to play;

We sat still and listened for quite some time,
Going over the night's events, each in our mind;
We looked at each other and swallowed long and hard,
When it became quite apparent the cows were back in
the yard.

About The Author

Debby Schoeningh and her husband, Mike, live at the base of the Elkhorn Mountains in rural Eastern Oregon where they have a cow/calf operation.

Her writing and photography have appeared in the Western Horseman magazine, the Oregon Business Magazine and the Cascade Cattleman. She continues to contribute to several publications on a regular basis including the Ruralite magazine and the Capital Press newspaper. She is also a writer/editor at *The Record-Courier* newspaper where she writes her column "The Country Side."

Debby enjoys the beauty of nature and spends her spare time photographing the ranching life and Eastern Oregon's landscape. Her work can be seen on the Internet at http://www.thecountrysidepress.com.

Tails From The Country Side

Published by

The Country Side Press
P.O. Box 34
Haines, OR 97833
www.thecountrysidepress.com

LaVergne, TN USA
24 June 2010
187239LV00004B/17/A